C700520057

D1420917

Renegades Rule
this Land

When four pretty brides-to-be are in need of an escort to guide them across the dusty desert where they are to wed a group of miners, everyone tells them that Jackson Blake is the only man for the job.

He has proven he can handle rustlers, bad men and border-jumpers. But can he master four pretty women, a band of deadly gunmen and a sun-blasted desert, all at once? Blake thinks so . . . but the Badlands figure otherwise.

Renegades Rule this Land

Dempsey Clay

A Black Horse Western

ROBERT HALE · LONDON

ISBN 978-0-7090-9013-7

Robert Hale Limited
Clerkenwell House
Clerkenwell Green
London EC1R 0HT

www.halebooks.com

Typeset by
Derek Doyle & Associates, Shaw Heath
Printed and bound in Great Britain by
CPI Antony Rowe, Chippenham and Eastbourne

CHAPTER 1

THE DEVIL'S OVEN

Jackson Blake set a leisurely pace as he rode up the flank of the high ridge above the switchbacks of Buzzard Gulch, where even in the late afternoon it was still blazing hot.

He'd worked his lone way south-west for two hours straight in stifling heat, laying a false trail. His shirt was plastered to his torso with sweat yet there was no weariness in his movements, nothing but total alertness in every inch as he approached the crest.

The place the horseman chose for his lookout was a natural niche in the crest of the ridge. Here, two bleached boulders stood leaning together

5

leaving a slot between them just wide enough to angle a rifle through.

Should gunplay erupt, a man posted up here with a weapon could cover the entire gulch below with the rocks offering solid protection against return fire.

Before stretching out to take up his shooting position behind cover, Blake first smeared his face with red dust then coated the barrel of his Winchester to dull the metallic sheen.

This was a man better suited by nature and character to attack rather than filling the defensive role he had chosen this late summer's afternoon.

The truth was Blake reckoned he'd just about had his bellyful of violence ever since badman Bart Nero had jumped him out by Monument Rocks the day previous. That explosive clash had left Nero dead and himself hotly pursued across the hill country by a vengeful brother Chan Nero and his dog pack of gunners.

Blake had chosen flight today simply to avoid more killing. But there was a limit to how far a man would let himself run, and he'd reached that point by the time he hit Buzzard Gulch.

If Nero was capable of tracking him this far and so close, then it was plain that gunsmoke was now the only way to resolve what young Bart Nero had begun at Monument Rocks.

He resumed his stake-out position behind the canting boulders to take a series of preliminary sightings along his rifle, covering the open spaces which funnelled down into Buzzard Gulch. He was confident that natural camouflage and deep boulder shadows would do their defensive work well.

The effectiveness of his cover passed its first test an hour later when a rock lizard scuttled over his motionless leg with no sign of alarm. Blake didn't move a muscle. He'd learned the arts of stillness and patience from experts. The Red Man knew everything about such skills and Blake had learned all the Indians could teach him during the violent days of his youth. . . .

It seemed quite a spell before the sound of hoof-beats came at last drifting across the gaunt ridges and shadowed gullwashes of Buzzard Gulch.

Blake felt his pulse quicken as he sucked in a breath and calculated time by the sun.

The landscape lay drowsing before him in the approaching twilight with no sudden upflight of startled birds or absence of reptile life, factors which might alert wary riders to his presence.

His mount was safely stashed away in a deep draw a mile south; the rifle was heavy and reassuring in his hands.

7

The riders burst into sight abruptly in a bunch with Nero instantly identifiable by his white horse and big hat. They came drumming onwards swiftly with an air of grim purpose, four gun-hung hellions with the killer stink coming off them like heat from a branding iron.

The motionless rifleman exhaled slowly as he identified them all: Lang Simeon and his bloody-handed henchmen. Their combined scalps would fetch two grand down in Cobb City – top bounty price in the whole territory right now.

Blake exhaled slowly. The horsemen showed no hint of suspicion as they followed his deliberately laid tracks into the gulch. If followed, that trail would lead them all the way to the rocky escarpment a mile west, beyond which it wound away leisurely for some miles to be lost eventually in the heat-hazed fringes of the Devil's Oven desert.

Blake reckoned that if any survived his first volley he should be long gone before they could recover and mount a pursuit. They'd also have dead to bury; he would guarantee that one.

He was momentarily distracted when an over-working imagination transformed Chan Nero and his scum-gunners into another killer pack from another time . . . another murderous place. . . .

That bunch had been of the same breed as this

. . . and he could picture them vividly – men without character or conscience riding as deliberate as death as they made their way down through the slopes of the Stronghold Mountains towards the Indian camp to rape and to kill. . . .

There were five of them then and since that evil day each in turn had come to die under Blake's vengeful gun. It was only when the last of the five had perished after begging for the mercy he had never shown another, that Blake had at last begun to heal.

Yet he was still aware of the scars inside him in that final moment as he snapped back to the here and now and fixed gunsights on Nero. It was a thrill to feel the tension of the trigger spring beneath his curving finger.

The outlaw was a split-second away from death when Blake realized with a jolt that old pains and hatreds were leading him back to kill in cold blood again!

He snatched his finger off the trigger as though it was suddenly white hot.

Heedless now of the receding clatter of fast-passing hoofbeats below, he rolled over on to his back to stare up at a darkening sky. Slowly the fierce rage began to ease with the sweat growing cold and clammy all over his body. Strange, he mused, but sometimes he might go days or even weeks without remembering before a moment such as this which could bring it all rushing back. . . .

By the time he reached his horse twenty minutes later and with the hellions by now long gone, he was whole again. But Blake the iron man was suddenly made conscious that he'd been alone in the wilds and in danger far too long. What was really needed now wasn't gunfire and bloodshed, rather such healing factors as companionship, cold beer and a roof over his head.

And time – lazy time. . . .

Swinging away east in a huge semi-circle the lone rider eventually straightened his course and headed due north beneath a mellow moon. North lay Archangel. It wasn't much of a place but any lousy town sounded just fine to him tonight.

Crowbait Billy Johnson was growing impatient with the persistence of these pesky females. He grunted as he leaned forward in his battered chair there on the gallery of the Archangel Hotel, spat a stream of tobacco juice in the general direction of the horse trough, then scowled up at the four young women lined up before him.

'Ladies,' he drawled through a bird's nest of untrimmed whiskers, 'how many times have I got to tell you somethin' afore you get it straight? There just *ain't* no way across the Oven in July. They oughta told you that afore they sent you all the way out here.'

'They should have but they didn't, Mr. Johnson,' replied blonde and sassy Dixie Todd, swishing her parasol at a persistent fly. 'But seeing as we've come this far we certainly don't intend turning back. *Do* we, girls?'

Abigail Whitney and Beth Riley seemed as though they might not be too sure about that. But Carissa Carmody, the prettiest of these four mail-order brides who'd just been left stranded here in heat-stricken Archangel, supported Dixie without hesitation.

'We have husbands-to-be waiting for us across the desert in Tincup,' the girl announced to Billy and his bunch of porch loafers. 'They are expecting us by the end of the month and we're not going to disappoint them or ourselves either. Surely there is somebody here in this benighted hole who is man enough to escort us out there?'

This remark was intended to challenge the manhood and gallantry of the three men loafing in their weathered chairs, but failed.

Crowbait Billy, Thad Colburn and Ed Larsen had lived long enough in Archangel to have had any hint of pride or other virtues they may have once possessed baked out of them long ago.

Archangel was that kind of a town.

Larsen sighed wearily and shrugged while Colburn brooded down at his pipe, wondering if he had the energy to refill the bowl with shagcut. Only Crowbait was man enough to respond.

'It ain't jest a case of who is or ain't man enough, missy,' he drawled. 'It boils down to who'd be fool enough even to try. You see, the mortal truth of it is, you purty fillies just don't understand the country out here, you bein' from the East and all.'

He paused to sigh, and jerked a gnarled thumb westwards where the coloured fringe of the Devil's Oven lay like a shimmering yellow streak under a furnace summer sun. He inhaled audibly, regretfully.

'That there desert yonder ain't nothin' like most folks ever seen. Why, in midsummer even a rattler or an Apache is hard put to keep alive out there, and they is both bred to it. She's mean as poison even in winter that there desert – but in summer?' He whistled through his teeth and shook his sorry head. 'Well, I guess all I can tell you is that the early folks never got to namin' her the Devil's Oven without good reason, no siree!'

By this even sassy Dixie Todd was beginning to

appear a little uncertain as she gazed west. She turned to study her companions pensively before swinging back upon the old man.

'Well, is there a way *around* the desert then?' she demanded impatiently.

'Mexico to the south and badlands where no white man's never drove a wagon across far to the north,' Crowbait supplied drily. 'You might as well face it, ladies, you ain't gonna get no place—'

'I still feel you're exaggerating,' Carissa Carmondy interjected. 'Before we left Santa Fe I heard about an entire party of Mormons who'd crossed Death Valley unharmed just a few weeks ago. Are you trying to tell us this desert is worse than Death Valley?'

Crowbait Billy snorted derisively through his whiskers.

'Death Valley? Missy, Death Valley is just hell in high summer. But the Oven is hell, death and damnation for strong men and that goes treble for mere womenfolks. Sure, when you get to Tincup the real desert's behind you and it's green and cool, like your boyfriends likely told you. But gittin' there ain't for women, and mighty few men. So now why don't you little fillies stop botherin' us, accept that there ain't no way across the desert this time of year, and start makin' plans to go back the same way you come?'

It sounded like good advice.

By this time it was slowly dawning upon the west-bound quartet that their agent had been both dishonest and unscrupulous in not warning them what to expect upon reaching Archangel. Nonetheless, none of the party had any intention of quitting as the women showed as they walked away to make their colourful progress across the broad stretch of dusty thoroughfare that passed for Archangel's main street.

For all were unusually strong-minded young women who for various reasons were prepared to gamble on the great uncertainty of becoming mail-order brides to affluent prospective husbands out here, as they'd been unable to snare any such back East.

The quartet had already endured five brutal days' travel by jolting stagecoach across some of the harshest country in all New Mexico in order to put three-quarters of their journey behind them.

Of course, they had already been warned by just about everyone regarding the proposed last leg, stretching from Archangel out to the ordinary-sounding Tincup across the desert known as the Devil's Oven.

Yet had they been the quitting breed they would never have set out on such a venture and were certainly not about to quit now.

The clientele of the Golden Gate Saloon were hard men to surprise or impress yet the sudden appearance of four dazzling young Eastern females managed to achieve both. Yet as that mixed group of drifters, hard-rock miners, loafers, cowhands and loners from places that didn't even have a name quickly came to understand, these women were all business and lost no time in putting the big question. Namely, were there any *real* men here able and willing to escort them across the Oven?

Surely they had to be joking?

The response was an unqualified 'No!'

Leastwise, that was the initial reaction before the girls found some small encouragement in the information that a local identity named Gold Teeth Jones had for a time somehow managed to get provisions out to the miners, among whom were their prospective husbands.

Gold Teeth was a muleskinner once freely regarded as the toughest man in the region, afraid of nothing and a desert man to the bootstraps. Prospector, brawler and squaw man, Gold Teeth had lived most of his turbulent life in the Oven for thirty-five years until his most recent attempt at a midsummer crossing of the desert had ended in his disappearance, never to be seen or heard of again.

The girls showed little interest in the story of Gold Teeth or his probable fate at the hands of some desert hellions known as the Raiders. The four saw themselves as a unique breed, independent, adventurous and totally committed to fashioning new lives for themselves in the 'exciting and fascinating Great West', as an advertisement had described it. They were responding to an advertisement lodged by a number of highly successful but women-starved gold miners out at Tincup, and had even agreed to marry them providing they proved as successful and rich as they advertised themselves to be.

In correspondence, the Tincuppers had pledged that their brides could run things however which way they might desire should marriages be the eventual outcome of their journey.

The debate continued for some time before the local hardcases and the almost-too-pretty husband-hunters were forced to take a break from all the talk. It was only then that everyone grew aware of the Raider horseman approaching along the street.

The girls didn't yet know that the flamboyant figure was known here as a Raider, but it wouldn't be long before they did.

He appeared to be somewhere around twenty-five, hungrily lean with a dark and dangerous face beneath a tip-tilted sombrero and forking a half-wild mustang. Loafing towners snapped alert but were silent as the rider clop-hoofed by, favouring the women with a stare that was half-hostile, half-curious.

The new arrivals had never even heard the term Raider up until now, but were quick to learn it was a name to be feared and reluctantly respected.

Dixie Todd favoured the passing rider with a frown of distaste, then tossed her hair and forced a smile as she suggested the town's eatery for an overdue meal with her companions.

They must keep their strength up no matter what, she insisted, with an attempt at cheeriness, even if it was plain by this that, what with the heat and wild-looking boy-men on horseback and the rest, the prospect of dining at the Buffalo Hump held little appeal. Yet they were starving and so headed off for the Buffalo Hump without delay.

They found the eatery almost clean with shutters on two of the three front windows closed against the worst of the heat and glare. The girls took their places around a little table with a checkered cloth and the Mexican who filled the roles of cook, waiter and cashier brought them coffee and took orders.

Pablo's special of the day was chilli con carne, but they settled for a large platter of surprisingly fine

17

sandwiches, and soon were ordering second cups of coffee while the conversation flowed easily again.

All had been dismayed by the raw reality of Archangel. At first. Yet by the time a relaxed half-hour had passed and they'd eaten well, they concluded that despite all the difficulties and disappointments they were encountering they were still unanimous in their resolve to carry on. They must at least get to meet their mail-order husbands-to-be, and so would persist until they'd secured a reliable guide capable of leading them out across Devil's Oven desert to reach the Tincup mining camp.

Ever since quitting Sante Fe, Tincup had been their only goal, and though they'd been made aware of the difficulties and dangers of their journey by this, there was no thought of quitting now. Not for any reason.

'All we really need to make the journey, as I see it,' Carissa Carmody said firmly after a brief moment of pensive silence, 'is the right man for the job. Whether we will find the right guide here in Archangel, however, seems uncertain, from what we've seen. So far, I'm not sure I've seen anyone I'd trust to guide me across the street, much less a desert.'

Heads nodded in sober agreement, even if some thought Carissa might be being over-critical. They found her to be generally dismissive of the entire male sex, whether they be encountered here or back in what she liked to term civilization, meaning the East. Yet she was still ready and willing to wed her mail-order man, providing when they reached their destination he proved to be as rich as she'd been led to believe.

All four were marrying for money. Each had tried and failed to find both love and money, so had sat down one day together and agreed unanimously that, seeing that they all wanted to be rich and secure more than anything in the world, they would settle for whatever fate might cast their way in the way of husband material out here – providing the almighty dollars were there.

At the saloon they'd been given names of various scouts and guides, but those interviewed so far had all fallen short of the mark for any number of reasons, dismally short. They'd heard of another Archangel scout with a high reputation as a guide, but as he wasn't currently available it was eventually agreed that they would simply wait until he showed; it seemed the only sensible course.

Somewhat cheered after this had been settled to their satisfaction, the group quit the eatery to head back for the hotel. The day's worst heat had eased and Archangel was stirring into sluggish life in the cool of the late afternoon.

They sighted Telly Priest and his three sidekicks from the Yellow Hills watering their pack mules across at the Golden Gate's water trough. Crowbait Billy Johnson and his pards hadn't moved from the shade of the hotel gallery, while down at the livery a tall man in a dusty denim shirt was leaning against his horse and yarning with the liveryman.

It was Dixie Todd who spotted this man first, and promptly brought the others to a halt by the peppercorn tree out front of their hotel.

'Now look at *that*, girls,' she said, primping at her curls. '*He* certainly wasn't around when we first began searching for somebody with even a hint of quality. You know, perhaps the longer we stay in this crummy town the better they get?'

The others paused to focus on the object of her attention and agreed instantly that this certainly had to be a huge improvement on anything sighted thus far. At well over six feet in height, broad-shouldered and capable-looking, with the lazy grace of an athlete, he looked loaded with potential.

'Mmmm!' Carissa murmured, then paused. 'But at second glance don't you think he might seem a little arrogant though, girls?'

'All the interesting ones always smell of trouble of one kind or another, honey,' Dixie declared with the air of someone who knew all about the male species worth knowing.

'Well, perhaps he's not exactly handsome,' Dixie commented critically. 'More rugged, wouldn't you say? Wonder who or what he is?'

They were still speculating on this when Beth Riley turned at a light touch on her arm, jumped back with a start. A lithe young Indian stood gravely before her clad in breech clout and leggings and clutching a bunch of flowers in a bronzed hand.

'Dixie!' she gasped, backing up. 'What does he want? Don't let him touch me.'

'Get away from us, you savage!' spirited Dixie ordered. 'What do you mean, scaring decent women like that?'

The young Indian seemed puzzled. Burns Red was a member of the peaceful Pima tribes but these strangers weren't to know that. To them, he looked exactly like a wild savage might, and they found his sudden approach alarming.

A sudden silence fell across the staring street. For in this race-tainted outpost Indians never approached a white woman uninvited, something innocent Burns Red was about to discover.

CHAPTER 2

THE GUILE OF WOMEN

Upon finally realizing the young Indian intended no harm, Dixie Todd forced a half-smile. 'You seem to draw all the wrong kind, honey. Maybe you'd better take his flowers just to make him happy.'

Before a nervous Beth could respond in any way, a whiskey-thickened voice sounded close by.

'What the hell do you think you're about, Redskin? You loco thinkin' you can go about scarin' white womenfolks that way?'

Without waiting a response, barrel-bodied Telly Priest swaggered forward and jammed a hard forefinger into Burns Red's rib-cage. He winced.

'Go on, beat it, buck. Get on back to the boon-docks where you belong!'

The Indian looked confused. Red was just a little simple-minded and all in Archangel, Priest included, knew it.

'For her,' Burns Red explained, holding up the flowers.

His incomprehension affronted the white man – an easy man to rile when in his cups. With a curse he slapped the flowers from the Indian's hand and shoved him roughly. He cocked a meaty fist.

'Uppity and stupid both,' he slurred, and began to swing a punch.

Burns Red made no attempt to defend himself as the big fist blurred towards him. But before that blow could land the tall, hawk-faced man from the livery stepped between Dixie Todd and and Carissa Carmody to block the intended blow. The miner whirled, cursed on recognizing the man, swung a punch from the hips. He missed his target and next moment was crunched by a vicious right hook that appeared to travel less than a foot before exploding against his jaw.

It was a blow to fell an ox, yet somehow tough Telly Priest retained his footing. With crimson trick-ling from his mouth the miner staggered, caught his balance, spat a vicious curse then swung a punch at his attacker's head.

'Injun-lover!' he roared as his opponent ducked low. 'What's this? Too yeller to fight, squaw man?'

Those watching the first real excitement Archangel had seen all week, saw Blake's dark eyes flare at the taunt. And Crowbait Billy Johnson groaned, 'That's tore it. Big Telly's just bought hisself a shirtfull of busted ribs I'm thinkin'.'

To the watching girls, Blake appeared both tall and well-made. Yet his opponent still loomed over him as he launched a vicious attack behind a whirl-wind of fists.

Blake deftly ducked and weaved with ease from everything thrown at him. He then brought Priest to a bone-jarring halt with a brutal right hook to the nose. Crimson splashed hotly and Priest's eyes filled with tears of pure pain. A volley of heavy punches to head and torso followed until the heavyweight's legs began to go. A crossed right hook jolted his head sideways and a left rip bent him double. Priest gasped in sudden fear and began to strangle as Blake hauled him up by his twisted shirt collar.

'Tell the man you're sorry, Priest!' he panted in the big man's sorry face. 'And mean it!'

A battered and scared Telly Priest was barely able to raise a croak.

'I'm right sorry, boy . . . I never meant to—'

He didn't finish as Blake released him and knocked him off his feet with a casual shove. Dust was still billowing up from the miner's sprawled form as Blake moved across to the wide-eyed Indian.

'You all right, Burns Red?'

The Indian nodded. 'Me all right, Blake. Me strong.'

Blake grunted and swung to face the crowd.

'Maybe that'll be a lesson to the rest of you.' He jerked a thumb over his shoulder. 'Indians have got as much right here as anybody else . . . more, if it comes right down to cases.'

He paused momentarily, inviting argument. There was none. He turned to the wide-eyed girls, offered a curt nod and started off across the street.

'*That's him*!'

Dixie Todd's excited cry startled her friends as they stood watching the man stride away, prompting her explanation.

'What I'm saying is that obviously is *exactly* the very man we've been looking for to guide us, girls. Surely it stands out a mile.' She swung upon barkeeper Toby Dence. 'That is the Mr Blake you told us about at the saloon, is it not, Mr Dence? One of your so-called desert men?'

'That sure enough is him, miss,' Dence responded. 'But I wouldn't try talkin' business to him right now

25

if I were you. Not in the mood he's in.'

But impetuous Dixie Todd wasn't about to be discouraged and insisted again to her party that this was plainly the man they were searching for.

Yet still stunned by the sudden violence they'd just witnessed, her companions weren't so sure, but when impulsive Dixie called to Blake and started quickly across the street after him, there was little option for them but to follow.

They did so slowly and uncertainly.

'What?' Blake's tone was abrupt when the girl reached him and tugged at his sleeve.

Dixie appeared neither intimidated or impressed. 'Mr Blake, I am Dixie Todd and these girls are my—'

'I know who you are,' he interrupted. 'You're the mail-order brides who got stranded here after the stage dumped you.' Blake appeared unimpressed either by her fresh-faced charm or her problem as he stared across the street as two towners toted the unconscious Priest away. 'So, what is it you want?'

The girl took a deep breath which did interesting things to the bodice of her snug-fitting green dress. Her companions took their lead from her by breaking out into smiles which were intended to charm yet seemed to affect Blake not at all. Nonetheless Dixie continued to smile and spoke up confidently.

'Mr Blake, you are the man claimed to be the

finest scout and trailsman in these parts, are you not?' she said charmingly.

'Could be.'

'And you know the Devil's Oven intimately?'

'You could say that.'

'Well then, I'm sure you would be happy to accept a contract to—'

'Wrong!'

Dixie's face fell. 'But, Mr Blake, you didn't even allow me to finish.'

'You were going ask me to guide you out there.' His tone was brusque. 'And judging by all the smiling and simpering going on, you figured I'd say yes.' He made a dismissive gesture. 'Forget it.'

'But, Mr Blake,' Abigail Whitney began, 'we need to hire the best—'

'Whatever you need is something I can't supply, miss,' he cut in curtly as he spun on his heel and strode away.

'Well . . . that is that!' Abigail sighed. Then with a sniff, 'I suppose he has his reasons for turning us down, but I must say I found him rather rude.'

'He strikes me as a man who has suffered some great sadness in his life,' opined blonde Beth, always ready to see the dramatic in everyone. 'I'm sure I could see pain in his eyes, I really could.'

Carissa Carmody's pretty lips curled as she followed the scout's receding figure with a scowl. 'The pain is what Mr Blake gives me – in the neck!' she said spiritedly. 'Men, they're all the same! Come along, we can do better than him!'

But Dixie Todd stood her ground and shook her head, her expression thoughtful as they watched Blake recede from sight.

'No, Carissa, they're not all the same,' she countered. 'I sense our Mr Blake is merely in a grump about something and is not nearly as forbidding and uncivil as he might seem. But I'm even more certain now that he is exactly the sort of man we need, and even though he said no, I don't believe that he really meant it.'

Beth Riley smiled at the older woman with amusement and affection. 'Don't you ever know when something is hopeless, Dixie? Don't you ever give up?'

'Never. And just between you and me, girlies, I haven't given up on Mr Stiff-Necked Blake yet. Not by a long shot.'

She sounded as though she meant it.

The searching night wind shifted direction, rattling specks of gravel against his boots as the moon shone down over the Devil's Oven with an eerie, crimson light.

Jackson Blake stood upon a giant rocky shelf which jutted sharply out into the sand, his wide-shouldered physique silhouetted against the backdrop of Archangel, an untidy scatter of gloomy buildings sprawled about hotel, saloon and store with yellow patches of light showing here and there.

A wolf howled some place far off over the desert, its voice rising higher and higher on eerie notes until it faded to become indistinguishable from the low moan of the night wind.

A crooked grin worked Blake's features under the deep moonshadow of his hat. He could envisage that wolf out there, likely perched atop a high ridge as he howled his challenge at the night, trying to convince both himself and all that heard him that he was master of this cruel country and wasn't afraid.

Blake understood.

For there had been many a time when he had been out there alone in the dark, reassuring himself that, like the wolf, he too had mastered the cruel Oven. While knowing deep down that neither man nor wolf, rattler nor gila monster ever managed to do so.

Not completely.

Jackson Blake loved the desert as much as he respected it and had the sense to fear it. Out there a man's life was reduced to fundamentals . . . earth, sun, water. There was no room for pretence or deceit. Out there. . . .

He turned his back to the insistent push of the wind while he built a cigarette. He'd been alone at the lookout for almost an hour ever since giving the Eastern women his firm and irrevocable 'no'.

They'd proven unusually persistent in the wake of his dust-up with Telly Priest at the hotel. That gabby blonde, Dixie Todd, had even come to his room half an hour after the brawl with a firm offer of five hundred dollars – their combined resources – to guide them out to Tincup.

The same girl had realized earlier that pretty smiles and fluttering eyelashes couldn't reach him. By the time she'd quit his room, she'd also discovered that it took more than money to induce him to agree to anything he regarded as reckless and maybe suicidal.

Scout, guide and trail boss to a bunch of giddy females across the desert in high summer? She must be joking!

Yet they were deadly serious, all four of them. High-spirited, educated and ambitious, with little respect for the entire male species, this bunch of old friends had recently been rudely made aware that all were in their mid-twenties and still single, almost over the hill, or so they imagined.

But the reality of this situation was that each one was merely uncommonly choosy and particular when it came to romance and it had seemed back then that they could eventually be doomed to become pretty but picky old maids if they either failed to lower their standards or agreed to settle for marriage without money.

They would rather die first!

Unexpected help and inspiration had come out of the blue in the form of an advertisement lodged by a group of gold prospectors and successful miners from some unknown outpost named Tincup, 'out West'. These women-starved diggers proved to be genuinely hungry for women's company – and very much able to pay to get it. So time had seen them arrive out here at the desert's very rim, only to find themselves stranded by their inability to secure the breed of guide and escort they required.

The two prettiest ones had tested Blake out next, without results. The youngest, Beth Riley, had said little, though there had been something about her shy manner and vulnerability that had almost caused Blake to weaken. Carissa Carmody had done most of the talking, explaining how desperately they needed to complete their journey and how they'd burnt their bridges and all the rest of it.

Blake was actually impressed by the way that handsome girl spoke up. She had not attempted to flatter him but rather gave the impression she found the entire male species something to be suffered and endured, just like the heat and dust. But even though the approach of the other two was different from the Todd girl's, the answer had still been the same. No.

Abigail Whitney was last to approach the unwilling veteran while he was busy sluicing trail dust from his throat with several jolts of Toby Dence's bad booze. Abigail was the party's last hope and set out to convince the trailmaster they were now desperate enough to provision a couple of wagons themselves and set out without a guide of any kind, should he refuse to help them. There were tears in the girl's eyes when she left, but Blake had seen too many tears in his lifetime to be either impressed or moved.

With his cigarette finally going to his satisfaction, Blake returned his total attention to the desertscape and let his gaze drift over south.

He was no longer thinking about mail-order brides but rather of a yellow-eyed *hombre* in a buckskin jacket accompanied by a trio of owlhoot-hardened henchmen.

He speculated on just how far Chan Nero might have journeyed out into the Oven searching for him when he was out there on his last job. He doubted the hardcase would have travelled any great distance, for he would fear the posse could have picked up his trail from Monument Rocks. Blake reasoned that if Sheriff Strat Spooner had stumbled across Bart Nero's corpse, and accurately read the sign at the Rocks, he would not have much trouble figuring out what had taken place nor why he, Blake, had been unable to return to the posse.

It was only by chance that Blake had joined Spooner's Cobb City bunch at Mitchell's Creek three days earlier.

He'd been on his way north after guiding a Mormon party down through Georgia Pass when he'd met up with that posse.

He'd worked with Spooner in the past and the lawman had immediately invited him to trail scout for this posse. Blake wasn't interested – until he discovered that the Nero bunch had slaughtered a rancher's family during a horse-thieving raid along the Little Snake. He instantly made himself available and had ridden with the posse until he and the sheriff disagreed over the direction the killers had taken from Buffalo Rock.

The posse had gone on north while Blake rode west, with the result that he'd jumped the bunch at Monument Rocks, killed Bart Nero, then led the others away to shake them off eventually at Buzzard Gulch.

From there he might have cut back east from the gulch to hunt for Spooner again, had he been a genuine manhunter. He didn't regret his decision to head north for Archangel instead. Sure, the whole Nero bunch deserved to be wiped out but he was willing to leave that task to those whose job it was to kill.

His cigarette transcribed a brief crimson arc as he flicked it away into the sand. He stood motionless staring out over the silent desert for some time longer before turning and making for the town.

He was feeling more relaxed right now.

He'd been played-out and empty upon hitting Archangel in the late afternoon and that set-to with Priest hadn't helped any. As well, those women had done their damndest to ensure he wasn't given any time to relax afterwards. But he'd just put himself outside a fine meal at Pablo's followed by a stiff whiskey which had helped iron out a few of the rough trail kinks from his spine.

This quiet hour on the desert edge was the ideal opportunity to slow down and loosen up.

Maybe after another couple of quiet shots at the Golden Gate he would be ready to grab some serious blanket time?

German Jack's house appeared on his left as his boots crunched on the gravel that marked the end of the made section of the street. From a building came a bull voice: Voman, you will be havink supper ready for me ven I am gettink home, and I will be gettink home whenever *I* decide to be gettink. You understand, *ja*?'

'Go, stay, or die with your boots on, you beer-bellied Hun!' came the ready response. Mrs German Jack had worked at the Golden Gate before the nuptials. She could, and frequently did, whip undersized Jack one-handed.

'Ho, hoh, I was only for jokink, my darling. Vere is your sense of humour, heh?'

'I lost it the day I carried you over the threshold, you drunken bum!'

Jackson Blake nodded, moved on. He would bet serious money that the only supper German Jack might expect tonight would be cold shoulder and hot tongue.

He was passing the livery stables when he sighted a familiar figure hurrying down the street towards him from the direction of the hotel. Big hat flopping and arms swinging, Mesquite Mick McGuire appeared to be in a big hurry. The runty trail cook's whining voice crackled sharply down the street as Blake passed beneath one of Archangel's street lamps.

'Hell, there you are at last! Damnit, but you're a hard man to find.'

Blake halted with a half-grin as the little man came stamping across to join him. 'What's got you riled up?' he queried. 'You run out of drinking silver again?'

'Very goddamn funny, Mr Blake. Where the tarnation have you been?'

'Here and there. What's wrong?'

Mesquite jerked a thumb over his shoulder. 'Them goldurned womenfolks is what. They—'

'Let me guess,' Blake cut him off. 'They've been working on you to try to get me to change my mind, right? Well, forget it, mister. I'm not—'

'There you go . . . jumping a mile ahead before you know what's underfoot. Will you let me finish – or is that asking too much?'

'Finish and be sharp about it. I'm dry.'

Mesquite sucked in a deep breath. 'They've hired Poole.'

Blake's brows hooked upwards in surprise. 'Tom Poole's agreed to guide them across?'

'Keerect. They offered him five hundred bucks

for the job, and you know Poole. He'd hang his own ma for half that.' He nodded with satisfaction. 'Uh-huh, reckon that's took the starch out of you some, Mr Blake?'

Blake didn't deny it. He had not taken the women's threat to cross the Oven seriously. Yet he was not surprised by Poole's decision. That bum would do anything for a dollar and would agree to take them out there for five hundred whether he believed he could get them across alive or not.

'Hey, where you goin'?' Mesquite shouted as he strode off.

Where Jackson Blake was going was directly to the hotel.

Damned females!

It was time they learned some facts about that desert and they were about to do just that!

With a muttering Mesquite trailing at his heels, Blake mounted the hotel porch and strode through the doors to find the four girls seated in the dingy lobby, almost as if they were expecting him.

He didn't pull any punches as he took up a position beneath the chandelier and told them exactly what they might expect should they even entertain the notion of making the desert crossing with a loser like Tom Poole. He went on to list some of Poole's more notorious debacles over the years then delivered a professional's rundown on the Oven itself – something they plainly needed.

He warned about the wandering Indian packs but mostly concentrated on a bunch of criminal white men known as the Raiders, who made their home out there on account they would be hunted down and hanged on sight any place else. He added a vivid description of heat and sand storms, the burning salt flats and the scarcity of water for good measure.

He wound up by recounting yet again the story of leather-tough Gold Teeth Jones's disappearance with all hands – never to be sighted since. That harsh lesson should be plain even for inexperienced females to grasp. If a man like Gold Teeth had failed to survive that crossing, what chance might a bunch of women and a guide with no sense of direction have?

Blake felt he'd rarely spoken more persuasively. Yet he might have saved his breath. They didn't even find it necessary to confer amongst themselves after he wound up. They simply traded looks then nodded to him politely before turning to Dixie, who rose to link her hands before her and survey Blake soberly.

'I'm sorry, but our decision is final, Mr Blake.'

'Damnit—' he began, but she spoke over him,

politely but firmly.

'However, we do appreciate your concern—' She paused to turn to her companions before continuing – 'however, due to your interest and the fact that we've had only the most glowing accounts of your trailsmanship, I know I speak for the others when I say that, despite your earlier refusal we would much prefer you to accept our offer. If not, I'm sure Mr Poole would—'

'Get you all killed!' he finished for her. 'That bum couldn't find his own way home in the dark much less—'

'Well, if you can't assist us then Mr Poole shall simply have to take us. Right, girls?'

Blake ground his teeth impotently but the sound didn't drown out Mesquite Mick's chuckle directly behind him.

'Looks like these here womenfolks got you on a griddle, Mr Blake,' the grizzled cook opined with some relish.

He swung on the runty figure. 'And who asked you, you broken-winded old cowpat?'

Mesquite shrugged. 'Well, it just seems to me that they got you licked, is all.'

'Licked? What the hell are you talking about?'

Another shrug. 'Well, you know you can't just let 'em go off with Poole on account we'd likely never sight any of them again. There ain't nobody else around, they's plainly set on makin' the crossin' . . . so what choice have you got?'

Blake glared at the man. Mesquite might be the closest thing he had to a genuine friend in these dark years following the loss of his wife. But the man was scheming, cantankerous and not even half as smart as he imagined himself to be. And if Mesquite expected Blake to knuckle under to the women rather than be responsible for what he saw as their inevitable fate he had another think coming!

Dixie's voice broke the silence.

'I'm very much afraid Mr Blake's mind is made up, Mesquite. Isn't that so, Mr Blake?'

Blake bit off a cuss word and let his gaze flicker from one pretty face to another. He was but a few short steps from the doors. He could walk right out and nobody would think any the worse of him.

So why wasn't he doing just that?

He broodingly suspected the answer to this lay in Dixie Todd's chin. It was quite a pretty chin – but that wasn't the feature that bothered him. It was the way that jawline was set as though warning him that once her woman's mind was made up there would be no changing it.

Nonetheless, he proceeded to argue, listing again all the solid reasons against the proposed journey both eloquently and persuasively. His words seemed to have no effect and he was turning on his heel to leave without a glance back – when time and recent memory hit him hard . . . the vivid, scarifying memory of another young woman who had perished when Jackson Blake had not been there to save her. A young woman he'd loved and could never forget. . . .

He returned to the here and now with a jolt and his face now appeared drawn and haggard. Something called responsibility was clawing at his insides while something contrary dragged him from the opposite direction.

He blinked and the full reality of the situation returned. He sucked breath and in his imagination was now envisioning the Oven and its limitless reaches in all its terror and stark beauty. He saw in his mind's eye the few isolated waterholes which only he knew as well as the Indians. The deep canyons and arroyos where even a desert man could get lost and perish . . . all the limitless scope and danger of a truly hostile environment.

And most clearly of all, he envisioned the real scourge of the desert – that dog-pack of white outlaws and killers known to roam its deepest reaches. Raiders. He mentally drew away from the sense of responsibility this awakened in him, yet it returned even more strongly than before. And treacherously he felt the tug of the great challenge – conquer the fierce Oven in midsummer – something no white man had ever done. . . .

His thoughts were interrupted by the thud of boot-heels on the gallery of the Archangel Hotel and moments later a gangling man with the face of a ferret walked in. Wagonmaster Tom Poole scowled on sighting Blake, then put on a gap-toothed grin for the benefit of the girls.

'Well, ladies,' he twanged in a thick Tennessee accent, 'I've got me a couple of wagons all lined up and Jobe Eastman's busy pickin' me out a few sound mules right now. So I reckon as how we could even be ready to pull out come sunup, if that suits you.'

Suddenly everyone was staring at Blake, whose expression clearly betrayed his contempt. Had the women been able to come up with an even halfway acceptable trailsman to guide them across the lethal desert, he would have been happy to see them off.

Maybe.

But Poole was a failure both as a trailsman, a citizen, even as a human being. He was a drunk and a fool and Blake realized if he ever wanted to enjoy a clear conscience again he must make a decision and make it now, before his instincts and better judgement overruled him again.

The words, when they eventually came, seemed to be fighting to remain unspoken.

'They won't be needing you, Poole. I'll, I'll guide them across.'

He regretted his words instantly and only dimly remembered the excitement which erupted in that stuffy room following his announcement.

'All right, all right!' he called, silencing them. 'That's more than enough of that. You can save your gratitude until you come down with your first bout of heatstroke, or until we all of us roll up to the first poisoned waterhole.'

He put on a fierce scowl as he fitted hat to head, but this only seemed to cause even greater excitement. He'd never known anybody to act so pleased at the prospect of heading into the desert to confront its midsummer fury and quite possibly – probably maybe – die for their trouble.

With a final disgusted stare around the excited room, he then headed for the doors.

'I'm going to see Eastman. Be ready at first light . . . not one minute later!'

He was on his way out when Dixie Todd reached out and caught his elbow. 'Thank you so much, Jackson – if we may call you that now. And I suppose we may, seeing as we're all going to be travelling together, can't we?'

'You can call me Mr Blake, Miss Todd,' he snapped, and beckoning curtly to a smirking Mesquite, strode from the room, tall in the doorway before he disappeared.

The girls turned wonderingly to Dixie Todd as the footsteps faded. 'Honey,' Abigail smiled admiringly, 'you really are a marvel. How did you know it would work that way? How could you have been so sure Mr Blake would not let us hire Tom Poole?'

'Just instinct, I suspect, my chickens,' Dixie smiled. 'I suspect Mr Jackson Blake likes to act tough and commanding, but right from the outset I detected a soft spot under all that seriousness. I just had to find it, was all.' She shrugged and winked.

'As you've often heard me boast . . . a girl can't win and lose three husbands without picking up a few hints on how to handle the male species, can she?'

She suddenly laughed and clapped her hands. 'All right girls, enough excitement and chatter for one night. It's time we caught our beauty sleep for we must be at our best when we see Mr Blake in the morning.' She struck a masculine pose and with feet wide-planted and hands on hips, managed a reasonable throaty imitation of Blake's voice. '. . . In the morning at first light . . . not one second later. Hear?'

The sound of girlish laughter carried out into the night streets of the desert town like music.

CHAPTER 3

OUTLAWS IN TOWN

He was ready to go.

He stood on the gloomy porch of Pablo Chavez's eatery adjusting the set of his flat-brimmed hat. On the other side of the window a sleepy-eyed Chavez was slurping from his coffee mug. Pablo had been dreaming of a wealthy, creamy-breasted and stunning *señorita* who wanted nothing so much as to make poor Pablo her lover and master of all her fabulously rich lands in Old Mexico – when Jackson Blake had come stamping in, yelling for coffee.

Pablo would never understand gringos.

By now the lights of hotel and livery stables burnt brightly in that dark, cold hour before dawn. He

46

could hear Mesquite cussing in the stables as he harnessed a span of mules. The cook had been full of sass and vinegar last night when they quit the saloon but was anything but chirpy when Blake had rousted him out of bed an hour before.

Blake made his way along the echoing, quiet street, pausing before the hotel to listen to the sounds of activity within. He grunted and continued on his way.

All about him now Archangel's few early sounds were familiar and reassuring in the morning hush. There had been many times when he'd walked this street in the pre-dawn hour with some challenging assignment stretching ahead, yet seldom had the sensation of leaving seemed so sharp.

But there was no real mystery as to why that should be so. He couldn't recollect having undertaken a job as dangerous and uncertain as the one ahead of him right now. This desert was truly a brute and it felt almost as if the very timbers and stones of the ugly little town were trying to tell him something, to warn that it still was not too late to change his mind.

Only thing wrong with that – *they* wouldn't be changing their plans no matter what he did. The women. He'd met stubborn and opinionated females aplenty in his time, but this bunch left all others in their dust.

He was half-grinning at the way his thoughts were running as he passed by the darkened Golden Gate. Maybe he should have passed up on that third mug of coffee? Caffeine over-stimulated, or so a medico he'd taken hunting once had told him.

He crossed to the stables with the silent, slightly pigeon-toed gait which was a legacy of the growing years he'd spent amongst the Indians.

The two lofty Conestoga wagons loomed dark and bulky against the lights. Mesquite and livery-man Jobe Eastman had completed the harnessing of one and were working on the second. Others were checking out the wagons, one laden with supplies and water barrels, the other piled high with mattresses and the girls' luggage. Mesquite yelled irritably for him to lend a hand but Blake ignored him and entered the stables to check on his saddler.

The big roan whickered a greeting and Blake drew out a lump sugar for him. He got busy and his chores were all but completed by the time a light footfall sounded and he turned to see the young Pima, Burns Red framed in doorway.

'Ho, Blake.'

'Ho, Burns Red. Howcome you're up and about? All this racket wake you?'

The slender Indian came in to stand by the

horse. 'Blake really go into desert?'

Blake was putting the finishing touches to his saddling. He straightened.

'Yeah, that's so.'

'I come.'

'Why?'

'Burns Red good scout. Blake know that.'

'I also know that any man has to be half loco to go out into the Oven this time of the year, considering the heat and Raiders.'

'You go.'

Blake half-grinned. 'Maybe that proves my point.' Then he sobered and added, 'Look, Burns Red, you know I'd like to take you along, only—'

'I not afraid. Pimas know desert.'

'Just a minute, mister,' Blake frowned as a thought hit. 'You're not offering to come because of that girl, are you? You know, the one you were trying to give flowers to yesterday.'

'She pretty.'

'Uh-huh, that's what this is all about.' Blake paused. 'Look, that is a white woman and you know they always spell trouble for Indians. Anyway, she's going out to Tincup to marry some miner, so—'

'I look after her, Blake. Maybe Burns Red, he look after Blake too? In desert are many dangers.'

Before Blake could respond Mesquite Mick came

tromping by, chomping on an unlit pipe. The camp cook propped when he sighted the Indian. 'What's he doin' here?' he growled. Excluding women and horses this man hated just about everything, with Indians high on the list.

Recalling last night at the hotel, Jackson Blake reached a quick decision. 'He's coming with us.' He grinned at the youth. 'Get your horse, Burns Red. I just decided I can do with an extra hand after all.'

The young buck's eyes filled with gratitude as he tossed a snappy salute and padded away, leaving the camp cook scowling after him.

'If you reckon I'm riskin' goin' into Raider country with just a greasy buck at my back, you got another think comin', Mr Blake.'

'The teams ready yet?'

'Of course they're damned ready. But what about that scalp-lifter?'

'Nothing about him,' Blake replied, and led his saddle horse out into the yard. He knew Mesquite was just sounding off, like always. A team of wild mustangs wouldn't keep that roughneck rube here in Archangel, much less one tame Pima.

The women had appeared from the hotel by this and were now assembled about the Conestoga wagons, inspecting them curiously and with some excitement. This was all just part of a great adventure for them, mused the watching trail boss. He found himself hoping they wouldn't be too disillusioned by the time they reached their destination.

The brides-to-be had dressed for the occasion in clothing they would find to be totally unsuitable on their very first day out. But they looked good and Blake noted that Carissa Carmody had chosen a split, knee-length riding skirt, her superb legs encased in soft leather tan boots.

Not for the first time the trailsman found himself wondering how this good-looker had ever become a mail-order bride. She was the sort most men anywhere would readily fight over – and he made a mental note to see nothing like that happened on his watch.

He nodded to the party as they went on by, then tethered the roan before going to check out the mules. By the time he returned, Burns Red had come back astride his paint pony, and Mesquite was yelling, 'Better watch out for your topknot, gals. Woo! Woo! Big bad Injun! Bad Raiders. Everybody very bad, and—'

'Shut that!' Blake snapped. He crossed to the women who were now eyeing the Indian worriedly. 'It's all right,' he reassured. 'Burns Red is really a friendly. He's also a top hand on the trail and can spell you ladies at driving from time to time. All right, it's time we got started.'

Reassured, the girls clambered up and Dixie took the reins of their Conestoga and six. Blake had few concerns about the women or the driving during the early part of the journey for it would be level going for most of the journey and most times all a driver had to do was keep the mules travelling in the right direction, which in this case, was west.

Dixie had told him she was an experienced driver from the days when one of her ex-husbands had a farm back in Kansas. She proved it by the dexterity she displayed in wheeling her team and rig from the yard and out onto the main stem.

Mesquite followed, driving the second wagon behind. He spat tobacco juice onto the rumps of the mules to show how he felt about women drivers.

Then they were rolling.

'Best of luck, Mr Blake!' Jobe Eastman hollered with a wave.

Blake nodded and rode up past the wagons to lead the way. It was swiftly coming on dawn. On the far side of town, a cockerel sounded and flapped his wings, briefly silhouetted against the slowly emerging horizon.

Soon the last houses of Archangel had drifted behind and the chilly wind coming in off a hundred empty miles was in their faces.

Blake's mount tossed its head as its hoofs touched the first stretch of sandy soil; the big roan knew the desert and could scent it ahead. The mules, fresh following some rest-up time and hand-feeding, tugged willingly at the leathers while the big, canvas-covered Conestogas swung away over the ruts and hollows like big-hipped, happy girls.

Jackson Blake halted his mount a mile out of town and watched the cavalcade roll on by. He built a smoke and set it alight, gazing back at the town. Was he loco, hoping to find peace and something more . . . out there? After a time he started out after the wagons and the roan broke into a trot.

The man at the bar of the Golden Gate had never been seen in Archangel before, and yet his face seemed somehow familiar. The reason for this was that his was a face they'd seen on the wanted dodgers a bounty hunter party had left there on their way south several months before. And now and then it might also appear in the newspapers that came in by stage, usually with captions such as NERO GANG ROB BANK! or CHAN NERO HELD RESPONSIBLE FOR MURDER!

It was not a face easy to mistake, with a hooked beak of a nose, the razor-slash mouth and the deep-set yellowed eyes of the true maverick.

They got to see any number of ugly faces around Archangel from time to time but Chan Nero's pan had to be in a class of its own.

The gang had dusted down the main stem that morning just as the Golden Gate was opening the batwings for business. Having checked out the town from the hills before venturing in the badmen were satisfied there was no law about and had come riding in openly and boldly. They already knew Archangel had no sheriff's office; their sole concern had been that the Cobb City posse might have found its way here ahead of them.

The outlaws hadn't sighted the posse since the brief clash with Jackson Blake at Monument Rocks, but the wily Nero wasn't ready to believe that the lawman had quit.

Sheriff Strat Spooner was a fool in many ways, but was also stubborn and persistent when it came to giving badmen a hard time of it.

It was Chan Nero's decision to make for Archangel after realizing Blake had foxed them down south. Lang Simeon reported he'd heard that Blake visited Archangel occasionally. That was enough for Nero who still had a blood score to settle with the man who'd slain his brother, Bart.

As soon as the hardcases had taken the edge off their thirsts the badmen began firing questions about Jackson Blake, only came up empty.

Archangel wasn't aware what bad blood might exist Blake and Chan Nero, but horse sense told the towners that whatever it was Nero wanted with big Blake it would not be to his benefit. Blake had few friends in Archangel yet there was still no risk they would sell him out to scum like Nero and his dog pack.

For his part Chan Nero wasn't sure if they were holding out on him or not. Weariness and a few heavy shots of rye had dulled his perceptions. Earlier, he'd toyed with the notion of shoving a loaded six-shooter under some random citizen's nose just to find out if he was telling the truth or not, but finally discarded the idea.

Whenever a man started cutting up rough in hick towns like this, they were bound to attract big trouble of one breed or another, and trouble was something they could well do without right now after a solid week on the trails.

Maybe . . . so he mused after they'd rested up some and stoked up on some hot and greasy chow . . . they might later feel more ready to put their questions in a forceful manner. But for now it was just good to stand in a cool bar-room and let their troubles simply ease away.

Drinkers wandered in and out, some casting a

wary eye in the direction of the dusty bunch at the back bar, for news of the gang's presence had swept Archangel like a brush fire within minutes of their arrival.

The town's more cautious citizens might have liked to steer clear of the Golden Gate that day, but with thirsts like theirs in a climate like this that was plain impossible.

Most tossed down a couple of quick ones and hustled off again, yet a hardier few, encouraged by the outlaws' seemingly peaceableness, had lingered. Already there was a six-man game of stud going on under that big oil painting of some lovely called Chloe – who was wearing no undershirt at all.

Chan Nero's yellow gaze was studying this work of art with deep interest as he sipped whiskey from a shot glass and scratched his lean gut with a dirty finger nail.

Isaac Orford and Lang Simeon lounged against the bar at his side passing derogatory comments on the quality of Toby Dence's booze.

Black-bearded Maitland Gwyn meantime nursed a beer out on the front gallery and kept both eyes skinned for anything or anybody that might show up along the street.

It wasn't until Nero had drained his glass and turned back to the barkeep for a refill that he noticed the big man with the battered face staring in his direction again. The outlaw caught the fellow's eye and held it until the man dropped his gaze again.

This time the hardcase scratched his head and rifled through his memory file. Within a short space of time the name jumped up for him. Priest! That was it. They'd questioned the drinker before, and Priest had told them he was a miner from the Yellow Hills. Judging by his scarred features and mean stare, mining must be a rougher business than he might have figured.

'Anythin' wrong, Chan?' asked buck-toothed Orford at his side.

'Mebbe, mebbe not,' Nero murmured, signalling Dence to fill it up again. 'But that ugly big geezer sure seems mighty interested in us.'

'Yeah, so I noticed earlier.' Simeon gazed at the miner who had taken to studying his cards intently of a sudden. 'You don't figure he could be nursin' some fancy notion about makin' a try to claim some bounty money, do you, Chan?'

Chan Nero laughed, a harsh, braying sound. 'A plugger like that?' he snorted. 'Not in a million years.'

Nero glanced up at the bar mirror. Priest appeared genuinely absorbed in the game now.

Orford started up about some hot-blooded Mexican dressmaker he'd known down in Sonora. Nero listened for a time and had forgotten about the miner by the time they quit the saloon some time later to make across the street for the eatery.

Pablo Chavez's place emptied quickly when the badmen jingled in, but they paid no attention. That sort of thing happened every place they showed. They stretched their legs beneath the table and dropped hats to the floor before ordering up a variety of dishes ranging from spare ribs for Maitland Gwyn to son-of-a-gun stew for Nero.

Soon they were eating, and Chan Nero grew increasingly silent and sombre as the meal progressed.

But the hardcase's worsening mood had nothing to do with the bill of fare before him. Nero had started in brooding about his kid brother again. Bart had only ridden with the bunch for three months and had only got to kill but one innocent citizen before Blake had blown his liver and lights out at Monument Rocks. He was bitterly reflecting upon the kid's lost potential as a real gunhand. He would have turned twenty-one next month. . . .

His thoughts were interrupted when Orford nudged his arm sharply. 'Hey, Chan, lookit!'

Nero scowled out through the window glass to

glimpse Telly Priest shambling towards the eatery. The miner was kicking a can before him and cast a large shadow. Priest hauled up on the porch to look around as if trying to decide whether he was genuinely hungry or not.

After a minute he passed a big hand across his homely features and shoved through the doors. He didn't glance at the outlaws as he took a table close to theirs. He ordered ham and eggs from the Mex then sat staring moodily out at the street while Pablo disappeared through the scullery door.

Only then did he turn sharply to Nero and hiss, 'What do you jaspers want with Blake?'

'What's it to you?' Nero countered.

'I ain't got time to bandy words, mister,' the miner shot back. 'You got trouble with that hard nose?'

'Mebbe,' Nero grunted. 'What if I have?'

'He took off into the Oven yesterday mornin' – that's what.'

Nero's yellow eyes narrowed suspiciously. 'Into the Oven in midsummer, mister? That sounds like hogswill to me.'

'It's the mortal truth. There was a bunch of women here with their fool minds set on on makin' it across to Tincup, and Blake agreed to take 'em.'

The hardcases traded glances. Orford began to

speak but broke off as Pablo approached and Nero growled, 'Get me another plate of stew, greaser.'

'*Sí, señor*,' Pablo nodded, and was gone.

'You levellin' with us, joker?' Nero hissed. 'On account if you ain't, then don't count on makin' old bones in this life.'

'I'm telling the truth,' Priest insisted. 'The women was stayin' at the hotel and Blake bought up the mules and wagons at the livery. You can check out what I'm sayin', but don't tell nobody I told you.'

'So . . . what have you got against Blake?' Nero wanted to know.

The miner's finger touched his scarred face. 'This. . . .'

Nero nodded slowly. Things were beginning to add up. He snatched up his hat and got to his feet, the others following suit. He stared down at Priest for a long moment then crossed to the counter, threw money down beside the register and headed for the doors.

'Señor?' Pablo's head appeared in the kitchen doorway. 'What about your stew?'

'You eat it, Mex,' Nero growled and the door banged shut behind him.

First stop was the hotel. They didn't inform the

jittery clerk what they were looking for, just swung the register around and checked out the entries. Four females had checked in three days earlier and all left together yesterday.

Next stop was the livery.

They had the scent of their quarry now and didn't care if they stirred things up some in Archangel now. Eastman clammed up initially when questioned, but loosened up when they kicked him around the stables some. Then he freely admitted that the party Priest had told them of had indeed set out to cross the Devil's Oven the previous morning.

Leaving Eastman swabbing a bloodied face, they sauntered outside to stand in the deep shade of the overhang and gazed westwards. In the distance, the Devil's Oven presented a grimly intimidating landscape of grey stone, yellow sands and a vast and bleached-out sky dominated by a big red sun.

Lang Simeon watched Nero uneasily for a time before breaking the silence.

'Anybody'd be plum loco. Have to be . . . this time of the year.'

'Is that a fact?' came the terse response. 'Well, pilgrim . . . we're going out there.'

Simeon's bearded jaw dropped. 'But Judas,

Chan, we could dry up and die out there—'

'Buffalo dust!' Nero cut him off. 'Blake's gone out there with a bunch of women and two big wagons. That means he'd just be crawlin' along – have to be. We can catch 'em up easy inside a couple of days and settle scores with Blake. And there's a bonus, too.'

'There is?' Simeon had the haggard look of a man who could use any bonus coming his way right now.

'Sure.' Nero exuded confidence. 'We can kill two birds with the one stone out there. We nail Blake, and we shake the posse for keeps. Even if that hard-nosed Spooner dogs us this far there's no way he's gonna take no posse out there in that hell country, and that's for sure.'

He sounded convincing, and Simeon's resistance faded in the light of his hard-edged assurance. He massaged his bony jaw, grunted several times, then spread both hands wide. 'Guess you got somethin' there, Chan.'

'I reckon.'

'So, when do we haul our freight, Chan?' asked Maitland Gwyn, trying hard to sound positive. This wasn't easy. He was no more enthusiastic about travelling the Oven than Simeon but wasn't about to contest the matter. That sort of thing could prove fatal when Chan had that look in his eyes that he had right now.

Chan Nero didn't hesitate. 'We pull out on sundown.'

CHAPTER 4

DESERT OF
THE DEAD

It was their second day in the desert. The first day out they'd encountered a pair of grizzled old prospectors at Sunset Springs, but today the Devil's Oven was devoid of all life.

They travelled slowly with the sun climbing their backs. Stretched as far as the eye could see in any direction lay a brown and yellow infinity of desert beneath a washed-out blue sky. They were following the dim outline of a horse trail that angled due west, horses and wheels raising a faint spiral of dust into the great silence.

Blake called a rest at noon in an arroyo beneath a rocky overhang affording protection from the sun. The three men unharnessed the mules, rubbed them down and fed them corn from the supply wagon.

They ate little themselves; it was too damned hot for food. Blake built a fire from fuel they'd brought with them and Dixie Todd fixed coffee.

She served it with a smile, something a sober Blake found quite remarkable. The others were all short on smiles, which Blake attributed to nothing more serious than plain fatigue.

Yet these women had spirit.

They'd displayed this in Archangel and were proving it again out here.

The sun slid two hours down the sky, the mules were led into the traces, and they were back out under the open sky once more.

Blake would have prefered not to travel at night but that was a gamble he could not afford to take. The prospectors had warned that the waterhole at Sulphur Flats was dry. So they needed to make the best speed possible in order to reach the next reliable water source at Dragoon Springs.

The mules began to play out in late afternoon and the party was forced to rest them again. It was still blazing hot, the sun a flood of infinite fire saturating earth and sky and sending billows of heat upwards from a blinding landcape.

They spelled until nightfall, then with the moon climbing from a sleeping earth, pushed on west again. Within two hours they had reached Sulphur Flats – and the dried-out waterhole.

There was human sign around the camping spot, and Blake examined it closely. The tracks were old, apart from those left by the prospectors several days past. There were prints of shod horses. Well-shod horses.

Blake sat squatting on his heels studying a single set of prints for some minutes before he was eventually joined by Burns Red. The young Pima got down on his knees to examine the prints closely, then gazed up into Blake's saddle-brown face.

'White man's horses, Blake.'

'Right. OK, time to get moving again.'

In the saddle once more, Blake led the party away from Sulphur Flats, his mood still deeply preoccupied. He knew that scattered Indian bands roamed the desert reaches from time to time, but had also heard rumours, and what sometimes sounded like solid fact, of a gang or gangs of white desperadoes roaming this vast desert landscape.

Indeed, it was these consistent rumours that had discouraged many a would-be goldseeker. His experienced eyes had failed to reveal what breed of redskin had been here recently. It could have been peaceful Pimas or nomadic Diggers. Then again, it might just as easily have been the human wolves of the desert lands, the Apache, or the Coyoteros the White Mountain Apaches, who came raiding on the plains.

A nerve began to tic under his left eye at thought of the Apache. His gaze swept their moonlit surrounds and his nostrils flared as he sampled the air. Jackson Blake prided himself he could smell an Apache at a quarter-mile; it was a never-forgotten stink of death that was forever associated with that dark day when the sky had turned black for him, never to be quite so blue again.

An hour's journey brought the party to a vast, echoing canyon. They travelled deeper into it with the trail gradually sloping downwards, the deep dust absorbing the sounds of the wagon wheels.

Another hour put the canyon behind them, and once again the broad monotony of the plains. A keen night wind blew in their faces, sharpening the sunburnt scents of the land about them. Mesquite dozed upon his high seat with hat tilted forward, jerking his head up every so often to curse his team whether they needed it or not.

Burns Red sat his paint pony, slope-shouldered

and relaxed off to the flank of the girls' wagon.

Driving her rig now, Beth Riley had her small hands encased in the pair of roper's yellow gloves Blake had given her.

Carissa Carmody sat at her side with one boot propped up on the splashboard and auburn hair tossing in the wind, while Dixie Todd and Abigail Whitney dozed fitfully upon the mattresses beneath the sheltering canvas.

The mules were moving sluggishly now, he saw. Blake too, was weary, yet his gaze never ceased its constant survey of rock, shadow and vegetation.

The party rested two hours at midnight then pushed on westward again until they realized the new day was upon them.

Mesquite Mick, as ineffectutal at judging either trails or distances as he was expert in the culinary arts, stared impatiently ahead as that red sun climbed. By his calculations he'd expected to sight the butte landmark of Dragoon Springs at sunrise but all that greeted his red-rimmed eyes was emptiness.

'How much goddamn farther to Dragoon, mister?' he bellowed irritably after they'd put another featureless mile behind themselves.

'We'll be there at ten.'

'What if there ain't no water there neither?'

'There will be.'

Blake proved right on both counts when the wagons swayed to a halt at rock-enclosed Dragoon Springs at five minutes before ten, and there was good water to be had. There was also sign. Fresh horse sign.

Sunlight shimmered on a basalt boulder where the skeleton of a gila monster baked.

From the deep shadows of the great boulders which marked Dragoon Springs, Dixie Todd gazed out over the sea of sand, stone and dust.

'The men've been gone a long time,' she mumured.

Abigail Whitney consulted her fine gold watch. 'Two hours.' She snapped the watch closed and glanced at Mesquite Mick who lay sprawled out upon a blanket a short distance off, chewing on his pipe stem. 'Should we be worried, Mesquite?'

Mesquite snorted through his whiskers. 'About Mr Blake? Heck, no. That pilgrim is just too blamed cussed ever to come to any grief. Why, I've seen grizzly bears take a close look at him then walk around him.'

'He did appear concerned about those tracks though,' Beth Riley reminded. 'I know he tried to hide it but I could see he was worried. Are he and

Burns Red trying to find the Indians who left that sign?'

'How would I know? He never tells me nothin'.'

They fell silent for a time after that, busy with their own thoughts. At last, Dixie clasped her hands together, looked wryly around at their surroundings, and nodded.

'Well, my chickens, I can only say – I hope they're worth it.'

'Who?' asked Abigail, though with little real interest showing in her pale face. This was their hottest day yet and it seemed to be affecting the girl from Maine more than the others.

'Why, those charmers we're going through all of this for, of course.' Dixie rolled on to her stomach, plucked a strip of dry grass from the sand and set it between her teeth. 'You'd think all this would be enough to cure anyone of the marriage bug, wouldn't you?'

Interest flickered over the faces surrounding her. Though a certain camaraderie had developed amongst the four girls since setting out from Santa Fe, it seemed they'd never had the opportunity to confide in one another regarding their backgrounds or their aspirations for the future.

Carissa undid the top two buttons on her blouse and fanned herself with her hat. 'What happened with your marriages, Dixie? Or would you rather not discuss them?'

Dixie Todd managed a pretty, world-weary kind of smile. 'Of course I don't mind, although unfortunately there's not a great deal to tell. For you chickens are looking at the absolutely worst judge of husbands-to-be found this side of the Mississippi. Do you know how long my last effort at matrimony lasted? Two years! And that was the record. Two years for number three, eight months for another, and – wait for it, girls – three weeks for number one!'

'You must be joshing us, Dixie,' Beth Riley smiled. 'How could you know somebody well enough to marry them, then split up after just three weeks?'

'You weren't listening, honey,' came the rueful response. 'Look . . . I always went just for looks. The moment I sighted a good-looking hunk I began smelling the orange blossoms. And number one was the best-looking – and the worst – of the lot!'

Her audience of three, plus the whiskery trail cook, digested the story for a minute.

At length Abigail spoke up curiously. 'But, Dixie, don't you feel that having had such bad luck with your marriages you must now be taking an awful risk in marrying some man, sight unseen?'

'Maybe not, Abigail,' came the reply. 'This Buck Miller I'm meeting sounds straight, sincere and honest – from his letters. He could be big and hairy but just so long as he's anywhere near the mark I know I can make a go of it. Let's face it, I'm not getting any younger.'

'You know, I really believe you will succeed this time, Dixie,' Beth said quietly.

Dixie's smile was back in place. 'Well, we can only hope even if we die in despair. Well, that's my little story. Who's next?'

Carissa, Beth and Abigail exchanged glances and eventually it was the latter who spoke up, condescending to relate how she had fallen for a wealthy young man of her own social standing back in Maine, and subsequently he took advantage of a business opportunity out West, wrote to her warmly several times until his letters stopped abruptly and she'd not heard from him in several months when she received a letter from him advising her that he'd married someone with money.

She felt unable to be an old maid and had set out West on seeing the ad for mail-order brides.

Beth placed a comforting arm about her shoulders. 'You'll be lucky, I know it, Abigail. What's the name of the young man you plan to marry?'

'Joe Dent,' Abigail supplied.

'You could do a hell of a lot worse, missy,' Mesquite Mick piped up. 'Them fellers out at Tincup are rough and ready, I'll allow, but there's scarce one of them who ain't a real hard worker. Yessir, they're an honest, straight breed, them cousin Jacks.'

'I agree with Beth, Abigail,' Dixie put in. 'I'm sure you will make it.'

Then her eyes turned to the youngest girl. 'Now what about you, honey? Is your story happier or sadder than ours?'

Beth smiled in her shy way. 'Rather sad, I'm afraid, Dixie. Poor all my life, had a boy who wanted to marry me who died – decided to come West. My man sounds nice by his letters and I'm so hoping he'll be something special . . . you know . . . sort of like Mr Blake. . . .'

'Ah hah!' worldly-wise Dixie said. 'I thought as much, honeybun!'

Beth looked flustered. 'What do you mean, Dixie?'

'I've seen you watching our Mr Blake, honey . . . with a certain look in your eye, so I thought. Not that I blame you. I think we've all noticed him because he's so confident and strong and—'

'For a squaw man.'

A silence fell as all stared at Carissa Carmody,

who'd interjected. The handsome woman smiled sardonically.

'Well, don't all look so disbelieving. It's just the simple truth.' She sat up and brushed dust from her skirt. 'Didn't you all hear what that miner yelled the day of the brawl at the hotel?'

'Why, yes we did, Carissa,' Dixie said. 'But I thought that was just some kind of insult. Surely you don't mean that—'

'I mean I was intrigued by what that miner said, and later checked up on it. Turns out Mr Strong and Silent Blake was married to an Indian, Beth. None of us has the right colour for him, which is why I believe he treats us the way he does. Sorry to shatter your illusions, honey, but that is the ugly truth.'

'Not exactly, missy,' rumbled Mesquite Mick, beady eye upon the girl now as he sat up. 'Mr Blake was married to an Injun gal once, but she died. Been dead a year now.'

Carissa arched a winged eyebrow. 'Does that make much difference, Mesquite. He's still a squaw man, and that puts him at the bottom of the scale out here, doesn't it?'

'To some, mebbe,' the old cook snapped. 'Not to me, it don't.'

'Nor to me,' Dixie said quickly. 'What happened

to Mr Blake's wife, Mesquite?'

'That ain't for me to tell you,' Mesquite growled, and turned his back.

The girls stared thoughtfully at the little man for a time. Then Beth said quietly, 'I can't see anything wrong in marrying an Indian girl . . . if he loved her.'

'You really believe in this thing called love, don't you, Beth?' Carissa said with a hard edge to her voice. 'Well, you have a lot to learn, sweetie. All men are the same, and you'll find this rube in Tincup no better than any other when you are Mrs . . . what did you say his name was?'

'I didn't say,' Beth replied, looking upset. 'But it's Felston.'

The colour drained from Carissa Carmody's face and her eyes appeared to stretch to twice their size as she stared dumbfounded at Beth.

'Did you . . . did you say Felston?' she asked in a voice barely recognizable as her own.

'Why, yes, Carissa, I did. Shade Felston is the name of the man waiting for me in Tincup.'

'Shade Felston,' Carissa breathed. 'It couldn't be—' She broke off abruptly, suddenly pale. 'No-no, I thought I might have known him, but I don't. That was . . . James Felston . . . yes, James.' She forced a smile. 'I'm sorry if I might have startled you, Beth.'

'You still look very pale, Carissa,' Abigal said, concerned. 'Can I get you some water?'

'Of course not. I'm perfectly all right. It wasn't what Beth said . . . it was just the heat.'

Dixie Todd was studying the handsome girl intently. After a silence, she spoke, 'You still don't appear well, Carissa. I-I don't suppose you feel like relating your story now, even though we're all just dying of curiosity.'

'Why do you say that?' Carissa asked sharply.

'Well, it should be obvious, honey. With your looks and figure you could land any man you wanted. You just . . . well, you just don't seem to be the regular mail-order bride type, I guess.'

'I guess,' Carissa said, getting to her feet. Her expression appeared irritable as she screwed up her eyes against the shimmering heat haze. 'Surely, it's about time Burns Red and Mr Blake showed up? What on earth could be taking them so long, Mesquite?'

The cook just grunted, plainly still miffed over what Carissa had said about Blake. Carissa shot the man a hard look then moved off some distance to lean against their wagon, staring out over the desert in the direction the two men had taken. Beth, Dixie and Abigail made several desultory attempts at conversation but the combination of mounting heat

76

and concern over Blake's protracted absence soon dried up the talk, until eventually they simply lapsed into silence to watch and wait.

It was almost an hour later when Mesquite Mick picked out the tiny figures of the two horsemen coming in from the south.

As the riders drew closer the effect of the heat waves bouncing off the desert floor caused them to appear to be riding on air ten feet above the ground.

By the time they drew into sharp focus they were within two hundred yards of the springs. They moved at the walk, Blake riding a little ahead of the Indian. The big man's face appeared stern and blank as he stepped down at the wagons, Burns Red appeared to be a little shaken.

'Well?' Mesquite snapped impatiently when Blake walked past him to drink at the spring.

Blake drank thirstily, then splashed water over his face before responding. 'We've wasted enough time here,' he announced, as if they were the cause of the delay. 'Break camp!'

This was an anticlimax following their tense time waiting. But they'd come to know their leader well enough by now to understand that it was pointless to try to question him on anything he didn't feel like divulging.

So all hands set about the by-now-familiar chore

of readying for the trail and within the quarter-hour the Conestogas were creaking slowly away from Dragoon Springs into the full yellow glare of the afternoon.

They'd covered a mile before Blake dropped back from point to let Mesquite Mick's wagon catch up. The old cook glowered down at him but he didn't speak. Blake covered several hundred yards with eyes sweeping in every direction, then without looking at Mesquite, said tersely, 'There was a party of six. They travelled five miles south of the springs, then veered west.'

'Why didn't you say so?'

'I'm saying so now.'

Mesquite spat a yellow stream of tobacco juice at a passing cactus, missed by six feet, cussed. 'Pimas?'

'No.'

The cook's eyes widened. 'Apache?'

'What's worse than desert Apache?'

'Coyoteros.'

The old man paled. If the Apache was the scourge of the desert, then the Coyotero Apache were the curse of the mountains. 'Six Coyoteros!' he breathed. 'Jumped up Judas! What are we gonna do?'

'We're going to make Tincup dead on schedule, is what,' came the terse response. And a grim

Jackson Blake kicked his horse ahead to leave the trail cook running stubby fingers anxiously through his beard. He'd been justly proud of that luxurious thatch for over fifty years yet for some reason it didn't feel either secure or reassuring as it had done just minutes before as he breathed the dreaded name aloud: '*Coyoteros!*'

CHAPTER 5

THE DESERT BREED

Beneath the vivid calico band holding his shoulder-length hair in place, the face of the horseman appeared like something carved from mahogany; imperious nose, cleft chin and broad cheekbones, a mouth as thin and cruel as a dagger blade.

Taliaferro the Raider followed the ant-like progress of the wagon train far below his lookout ledge impassively, until his gaze suddenly sharpened to focus upon the second vehicle, the one carrying the white women.

The desert man lay sprawled as still as stone atop

a high jutting shelf of sunbaked rock shaped like a giant water canteen. This huge slab thrust out from the flank of a red-walled slope a mile south of the wagon train where the hill's shadow reached out across the yellow plain.

In back of him his pack of killers squatted on their haunches with the lethal calm and patience of true predators.

There were five in the pack apart from Taliaferro. Duke and Murphy were both short and barrel-chested with such similar savage features for them to have been brothers. Ketch was no taller than the others but was broad of shoulder almost to the point of deformity, his ugly face made even more grotesque by the empty eye socket and the jagged knife scar running down the left side of his face from hairline to jaw. Hillburner was lean and stringy as month-old jerky.

In comparison with his henchmen, Florian looked like a giant among pygmies. He was even taller than Taliaferro's six feet and almost double his weight. There was no fat on Florian's sleek body and his skin was smooth as a woman's, whereas the others all appeared knotted and hard with muscle. The giant's expression never altered. He was as impassive eating an egg as he was blowing a victim's brains out at point-blank range with a Colt .45.

None of the pack had as yet caught more than a distant glimpse of the women's wagon train. It was for Taliaferro to study the situation then decide if they would attack or permit them to continue on their way. The predators had already been there under cover an hour in the heat, not speaking, rarely moving, as stolid and enduring as the cruel land itself. They could wait another hour if they must, or another twenty. None would complain. They were part of the desert.

A gust of wind brushed Taliaferro, stirring the flies which had settled on muscular shoulders. He didn't blink, move nor once take his eyes off the scene below.

The outlaw leader had been something once, an honoured and respected militiaman in the Desert Service. It was widely believed he would make colonel one day, perhaps eventually general, providing of course he conquered his great weakness.

Women.

A healthy interest in women was seen as a reassuring quality in young Service officers, but it was Taliaferro's obsessive lust which had finally seen him dismissed and black-listed first by the law and then by the entire territory. Until eventually there was no place left for him but the desert and the lust and killing that was a natural part of it.

That was two years before. In that time this wolf pack now known as the Raiders, had made their brutal mark upon the desert lands. There was a huge bounty on their heads, but the bones of men who'd sought to earn that reward were to be found scattered all over and bleached white by the sun while Taliaferro continued to prey on those who came to the deserts, wherever he might find them.

Yet it had been a long time since he'd glimpsed women of such quality here, if ever. White, young and pretty, they had at first sighting seemed as improbable and unreal as a mirage in this place and head-spinningly desirable.

It was only when he'd forced himself to check out their escorts that reality struck and the watcher felt his jaw sag.

For the two intruders escorting the women unmistakably possessed the look of professionals, meaning lean, sun-bronzed, gun-toting and dangerous. Neither one a tinhorn, it would seem. With quality mounts beneath them, rifles jutting aggressively from saddle scabbards and six-shooters sagging from tied-down holsters, the white man and the Indian looked about as formidable as anything a man might encounter.

It was a long and silent time before a brooding Taliaferro at length grew aware of the quiet surrounding him. He stirred and turned his head to find the others watching him with questioning eyes.

The pack comprised the survivors of various decimated desert gangs including the Coyotero Apaches which had finally gravitated around Taliaferro to prosper here. He had won their trust and confidence. A man always knew where he stood with him, both out here in the desert or back in the outlaw stronghold at Sharrastone, where they rested up from the raids and lived like bandit royalty.

Taliaferro was a strong leader whom a man could rely upon in any situation – unless women were involved. That could bring out the worst in him and more than one of his bunch began to sweat a little now as they watched him raise his field glasses to study the wagons and their glamorous payload yet again.

'Their outrider is big and wears a Colt like he knows how to use it,' he observed aloud. 'There is a Pima, an older gringo. . . .' He paused and his black eyes glittered. 'And three women, perhaps more.'

'What of the horses?' grunted big Florian. Horses to these men could rate higher than gold.

'Fine horses,' supplied Taliaferro.

'And you say . . . maybe three women?' Ketch muttered, licking dry lips.

Taliaferro nodded. 'It is a long time since I held a woman. . . .'

'And they are young?' Duke sounded as if he found this improbable.

'Young and pretty,' came the response as the leader raised his field glasses to his eyes again. 'And white.'

Doubtful glances were raised by this. Females of any description were all but unknown out here in the savage desert. The young, pretty and white kind sounded wildly improbable.

'I ain't never had me a young and good-lookin' white bitch,' confessed Murphy licking his lips.

'Well, that sure as hell's about to change,' Taliaferro predicted, inhaling to inflate his barrel chest. 'We ride.'

The six horsemen immediately quit the huge, odd-shaped rock formation serving as their lookout position. Soon there was nothing to be seen of them, with only the sound of receding hoofs upon stony ground to be heard. And finally, silence.

Mesquite dumped the soiled plates in the bin with a great clatter and reached for the water pail.

Moonlight spilled brightly over the camp set up in a draw, which was just as well as Blake had ordered no fires be lit that night.

Muttering and cussing about lousy chow and cold washing-up water, the crotchety little cook finally completed his chores before shambling across to the girls gathered before their wagon.

At the moment Dixie and Beth were singing, with Carissa and Abigail keeping time softly clapping their hands and swaying.

This was such a startlingly civilized scene out here in the raw desert that even leathery old Mesquite stopped to lean against a wagon wheel close by, nodding in time with the music. Until he turned and sighted Blake coming down from his lookout position on the rim of the draw, that was.

The old-timer pushed himself off the wagon and slouched across the canyon floor to meet his boss as he reached level ground.

'See anythin'?'

Blake was sober as he glanced across at the women, before resting the butt of his rifle in the sand.

'They're out there.'

Mesquite's eyes popped. 'Then you *did* see somethin'?'

'I didn't say I saw anything.'

'You're right, you never did. So, it was just instinct, then?'

'Right.'

'Well, mebbe you're wrong?'

'If I am it'll be the first time.'

The two locked stares. They wrangled a lot, trail boss and cook. Sometimes they argued over something important, but could just as easily get to disagreeing over nothing at all. This turned into one such occasion, until Jackson Blake suddenly glanced sharply around.

'Where's Burns Red?'

'Sleepin'.'

'Good. I'll need him fresh and sharp to stand watch later. What's for chow?'

'I just finished clearin' up.'

'I'll have jerky and bread.'

'You wouldn't maybe like that with lobster and French dressin' by any chance?'

'I'll settle for what I ordered.'

Curses and insults drifted back over his shoulder as Mesquite stumped off for the chuckwagon. Indifferent, Blake took out the makings and built a cigarette with deft fingers. He was hatless and the moonlight gleamed from his thick black hair as he hefted his rifle before making his light-footed way towards the girls' wagon.

He halted half-way with head cocked to one side, listening to the singing, his unguarded expression momentarily relaxed. Then he moved into the light and spoke tersely. 'Too much noise!'

The singing ceased and Carissa Carmody glanced

up at him resentfully.

'Is there anything we *can* do, Mr Blake? We can't light a fire, we're not to move away from the wagons, and now you're saying we can't even sing.'

'If you really want to help you can all turn in.'

'It must be really marvellous to play God!' Carissa snapped, getting to her feet. She rested hands on flaring hips to face him defiantly. 'You do enjoy that role – don't you, *Mister* Blake?'

'Please, Carissa,' urged Beth. 'I'm sure he's only concerned for our own safety.'

'Thanks, Miss Riley,' Blake said. 'But I can fight my own battles.' He took a deep draw on his smoke, eyeing a defiant Carissa. 'Something's irking you, Miss Carmody. What?'

She pouted.

'Well, I think you should at least throw some light on what's making everyone so jumpy tonight. We surely have a right to know.'

'I didn't know anybody was jumpy, as you put it.'

'Of course you did.'

'Hey, steady on, honey,' Dixie Todd interjected. 'Mr Blake is—'

'Oh, hush up, Dixie,' Carissa cut her off 'We all know something is going on that we haven't been told about. Ever since Mr Blake and Burns Red returned to Dragoon Springs they've been acting

88

differently. They keep staring around as if expecting something to jump up every step we take. That means something is wrong. And you are lying when you say that isn't so – aren't you, Mr Blake!'

Blake had been challenged in no uncertain terms and was for the moment off-balanced. Then Mesquite sauntered across and thrust a plate of chow into his hands.

'Jerky and bread, *sir*!' he said sarcastically.

'What kept you?'

Mesquite's homey pan turned choleric. He was only appeased when Blake unexpectedly grinned broadly.

'Relax, old-timer. Like the lady just said – you're jumpy as a kitten.' Blake turned to the women. 'Matter of fact you're all jittery, and there's no call to be.' He started off, paused. 'Er, you can sing some more if you've a mind, just keep it down a little, will you?'

He drifted off to eat alone and barely heard Abigail say wonderingly, 'He *actually* smiled! Will wonders never cease?'

The chow was hard tack, but filling. Jackson Blake ate with one boot propped up on a boulder which stood some distance back from the line of tethered mules and horses.

The Carmody girl was right, he reflected. He was lying in his teeth when he told them there was nothing to be concerned about. Even so, he saw no point in alarming anyone about what he'd sighted just yet. Time enough for that if it became necessary.

The meal finished, he hunkered down to rub his plate clean with sand before toting it back to Mesquite's kitchen. The clean dish was a peace offering and the cranky cook accepted it as such.

'I reckon you was right, Mr Blake,' he conceded, speaking low so as not to arouse the Indian sleeping in the chuck wagon. 'Guess I am kinda jumpy.'

'It's the safe way to be when there's Raiders about. That's if they *are* about, of course.'

'You reckon you could be wrong?'

'Maybe, maybe not.'

Mesquite digested that. 'Well, whichever way she plays out, you can count on me, boss man. I might be jumpy but I sure enough ain't scared.'

'I know that, and I'll be relying on it.' Blake hefted his rifle and looped it over his shoulder. 'Right now, I'm going out to check on the animals. Then I'll stand lookout on that south rim a spell. See to it that the women don't raise too much racket and send Burns Red up to me around midnight.'

'Got you, boss.'

Upon reaching the remuda Blake straightaway discovered one of the mules had broken its hobbles. Working by moonlight he was able to repair the damage well enough to last out the night. That completed, he crossed to his horse to feed it a handful of sugar. As he stood stroking the animal's velvet muzzle he glanced across the campsite to see that the women had concluded their impromptu concert and were at last getting ready to retire. He frowned when he saw that one slender figure had drifted some distance from the wagons to stand gazing up at the sky. He started across, his frown fading quickly when he realized it was Beth Riley.

'Better go back, Miss Riley.'

The girl turned with a start. 'Oh, Mr Trail Scout. I didn't hear you coming.'

'That's an old habit I have. Some folks call it sneaky.'

'Well, this was as far as I intended going. It's such a lovely night and I just wanted to be alone to enjoy it for a few moments longer.'

'Then I'll move on. But don't go any further.'

'Oh, you don't have to go. Being alone is a little scarier than I thought it would be. You're welcome to keep me company if you can spare the time.'

He nodded and leaned. 'Being scared can be the

smart way to be, out here. And – sure, I've got time.'

He really hadn't. He needed to keep patrolling yet made no effort to move on. There was something about this woman that set her apart from the others. He'd sensed this from the outset and it had grown increasingly evident as the days went by. There was a refreshing candour and boldness about Beth Riley that was attractive, and he sensed she was able to cope with his sometimes brusque ways better than the others might.

There was a stretch of silence before he spoke again.

'You women have stood up to the journey better than I expected, Miss Riley. I meant to tell you all before but somehow I didn't get round to it.'

'We all appreciate what you've done for us.'

'You have no regrets? Taking all these risks, I mean?'

Her expression sharpened. 'None. We knew it would be hard and dangerous.'

'Yet you still were ready to chance it?'

'Of course. You see, Mr Blake, all of us had given up on the notion of marrying for love when we found that simply didn't work out. So we decided to marry for money instead, and our menfolk out here at the backside of creation are loaded. If we get killed getting to Dragoon Springs, or find them all dead and being eaten by cannibals, so be it. But if we find them rolling in gold and crazy to marry us, then it will have all been worth it.'

'What about love?'

'What about it?'

'Where does it come in?'

'It doesn't. We marry them, brighten up their dreary lives, stay on long enough to relieve them of every last dollar we can get our hands on, then hire someone just like you to get us safely back to civilization to catch the first luxury train east.'

She smiled impishly and fell silent with arms folded as she turned to gaze up at that bloated desert moon. Maybe Blake should have been shocked by her candour, but wasn't. It could be a hard life in the far west. A man – or woman – did what had to be done to make a life and stay alive. And it was with a sudden jolt that he realized he deeply envied whichever miner got to share this girl's' life . . . even if that did prove to be just for a short time.

'Well, good night, Miss Riley. Don't stay out here too long.'

'I'm ready to go back now.' She smiled. 'I haven't shocked you, have I?'

'Not at all.'

'Then goodnight. Take care.'

Take care. Simple words. Yet they seemed to be more than dust that. How long was it since anybody had cautioned tough Jackson Blake to take care, he pondered, as he ascended the canyon wall. Seemed so long ago that he couldn't rightly recall if indeed it had ever happened. Folks just seemed to assume automatically that he was someone who could look out for himself.

He felt weary yet his thoughts were busy as he began pacing out his lookout beat high upon the canyon rim later. With the night wind whispering about him as he walked away the lonely hours he watched that big moon fatten and turn white.

When Burns Red came up just after midnight the Indian insisted Blake returned directly to camp to sleep. Yet even though he felt even more weary than before, Blake knew that for some reason his brain didn't feel ready to shut down, either now or later.

At least he did get to stretch out to rest his legs while the Indian paced the rim. It was some half-hour later as he sat staring out over the sleeping world that he picked up a faint flicker of movement upon the crest of a broken-backed ridge a hundred yards distant.

Blake rose silently. It could have been a wolf out there in the night, he reasoned, a bobcat or maybe a chipmunk. Yet every instinct warned it was a man.

Totally alert now, he knew he had to *know* what it was out there on that ridge, not simply guess.

He signalled Burns Red up to join him, told him what he'd seen and what he planned to do. Moonset seemed a long time coming but when it did he was ready.

Discarding boots and shell belt he stood in socks, pants and shirt with a cocked six-shooter in his fist. He'd coated himself liberally with dust, face and hands both. So prepared, he ghosted off into the gloom making no more sound than a moon shadow flicking across the face of the night, and by the time he'd covered just fifty yards the watching Burns Red could no longer distinguish his tall silhouette.

He'd become part of the night.

CHAPTER 6

LIFE AND DEATH

He covered the first half-mile at that same swift, distance-eating lope which he'd first learned and mastered during a boyhood shared with the Digger Indians.

Eventually, he dropped back to a jog-walk to cover the remaining distance which brought him to a stand of giant saguaro, his objective now less than a quarter-mile distant. The wind was blowing directly towards him and so should carry his scent and any sound he might make away from the ridge.

It took longer to cover those final few yards than it had done his entire approach, for he was now forced to proceed in a stealthy crouch and watch every step. He would cover three or four yards then halt in the gloom to listen and scent before satisfied it was safe to push on.

At last he gained the high ridge where he halted to stretch out belly-flat between sheltering boulders to watch and listen. There was nothing to be heard here but the brush of the nightwind, no sign of life but the occasional scuttle of tiny foraging creatures.

He let another uneventful ten minutes slide by before he rose and began to climb again.

This was the perilous part. If there were Raiders, Indians or any other deadly desert breed about, they might well hear him and kill him. He hated both breeds but had greater respect for the Raiders, the well-named vermin of the desert.

In midstep he checked.

For some time now the uneasy wind had been blowing east to west parallel with the ridge line. Now it switched abruptly from the south to bring the fresh scents of . . . sweat, horses, metal and gun oil.

Danger!

And freezing in his tracks like a man turned to stone, Jackson Blake's danger-honed senses sent his mind clicking back across the years. . . .

He was just twenty-three years old and on his way back home to the Digger Indian Valley, New Mexico

Territory. That was the place where he'd been reared following his rescue by the Diggers from the Apaches who'd slaughtered his family and abducted him to be reared as a fighting brave.

He had quit the Apache valley upon reaching manhood three years earlier to make his way back into the white man's world, but had returned just months before to marry his childhood sweetheart, Judy Red Girl, daughter of Chief Blue Elk.

It was the first time he'd left her for more than a few days at a time, when hired by the Army as lead scout on a punitive raid against the Apaches. He'd returned home eagerly through the green forests to their lodge on Blue Sky Lake . . . where that evil stench poisoning the clear mountain air was the scent of death. . . .

She had died fighting the Raiders . . . and in the fullness of time her killers had fallen under his vengeful guns. It had taken six months to find and kill them all and he'd never returned to Digger Valley since. She was still with him, likely would be forever. . . .

He returned to the present with a jolt and stared down at the six-gun in his fist. Six bullets, six Raiders. He knew where to locate the bunch which had left their sign back at Dragoon Springs. It was composed of a dog pack of white desert renegades and the Coyoteros, their slinking Apache hangers-on.

Together they'd slain Judy Red Girl and he'd never really looked at another woman in all that time since until. . . . He straightened sharply. What in hell did he mean by *until?* Nothing, he decided quickly, and was swiftly on his way.

He was inching up the slope before he realized where emotion was leading him.

Six bullets cutting down six killers would not be the clean mathematical way things would pan out, he knew. Couldn't be. If driven to act in blind anger he might kill some, then the others would kill him. And after that, Mesquite, Burns Red and the women would all fall into murderous hands like ripe plums. . . .

The brief internal struggle between anger and self-survival brought him out in a flood of sweat. But in the end it was Blake the veteran who triumphed over Blake, the man with a haunted past. 'Not right now,' he lectured himself as he inched backwards the way he'd come. 'There'll be another time and place for killing, Blake, there always is if a man is patient enough. . . .'

By the time he'd returned to the giant cactus his emotions were harnessed and he was able to view the situation calmly.

That there were Raiders trailing the party there could now be no doubt. Just as there was no questioning that they would eventually attack. So he could either wait for danger to find him . . . or he could do just what he'd always done.

Carry the fight to the enemy.

He stood alone and motionless for a long time as he conjured up and rejected one attack plan after another. Until he finally knew what he would do.

Dawn stole by grudging grey stages across the Devil's Oven. Gradually, the shadows of night withdrew before the light of the new day until at last the Raiders could see all the way down to that place upon the flats beyond the canyon where a sharp flurry of sudden gunfire had erupted half an hour earlier.

The killers sighted the horse quite clearly but it was some time before they realized that what had looked like a boulder near the animal's legs was actually the body of a man. The figure lay motionless. They identified it as the tall, tough-looking *hombre* they'd sighted leading the wagons the day before.

They traded silent stares before focusing upon the east again where a cloud of dust now rose sluggishly against the light. They'd heard the sound of wagons quitting the canyon following the clash of guns earlier. Their quarry became visible now as it rolled away westwards, yet was now without that tall rider at the lead as before.

Uncertain minutes passed in silence before Taliaferro spoke up. The Raiders still retained the same position on the broken-backed ridge they'd occupied overnight to spy out the wagoners' camp. Ketch and Hillburner had urged Taliaferro to attack during darkness but he'd had other plans.

He was in command. They would attack when he decided, not before.

Now he conferred some distance apart with Duke and Murphy for a spell after which the two gunners headed off down to the draw where their mounts were tethered. The pair swung up lithely with rifle barrels glinting, to lope over the high ridge and head off for the flats.

From distant cover, Jackson Blake glimpsed the riders briefly outlined against the sky before they vanished beyond the crest of the ridge, heading his way. Beneath his body the Winchester and six-gun lay in the depression he'd scooped in the earth before first light. He now lay sprawled as though dead with left arm carelessly outflung but with the right tucked beneath his body clutching the walnut handle of his six-gun. The ketchup he'd had

101

Mesquite splash over the back of his shirt earlier was slowly drying out, yet still looked convincingly like blood.

He was the bait to tempt the desert vermin.

One half-opened eye was the only hint of life in his dust-covered face as he watched the Raiders come slowly on by that same big cactus he'd stood beneath overnight. He counted two white men and two Coyoteros.

He'd hoped to draw more of the enemy in close in order to blast them all to hell. He desperately wanted to nail the pack leader, Taliaferro, believing that would swing the odds their way.

Right now, he was relying solely on the Raiders' passion for fine horseflesh to tempt the leader to come after the decoy of his big roan saddler, standing quietly tethered beneath a gaunt pine close by.

Suddenly he stiffened. Someone coming. Could one of these dim shapes be the leader?

The riders drew closer and Blake licked dry lips. The odds were still heavily stacked despite the fact that he was both geared up for action and had the drop. There was no difficulty identifying Taliaferro at closer range now. The bastard was impressive, he conceded grudgingly. It figured he would have to be in order simply to survive out here for any length of time. Yet even if they had the numbers he still believed he held the edge.

Just.

The riders suddenly halted their ponies just beyond six-gun range. They sat sniffing the air and muttering for several minutes before moving forward again. Blake saw no sign of life upon the ridge crest beyond as yet, but sensed the others had to be up there some place . . . watching. . . .

He felt a clear cold current course through him as the first body scent of the alien horsemen feathered his nostrils. His thumb curled the hammer of the Colt back to full cock and he was ready to kill.

Dead ready.

The party was within thirty yards when Taliaferro abruptly pulled rein again. The Raider swiftly jerked rifle to shoulder and found himself twitching in response to – what? Alarm? Suspicion? Instinct? There was no telling, but something had alerted this butcher.

Taliaferro's rifle barrel suddenly swung in Blake's direction and he went cold. Perhaps he did really appear dead, lying there, but the Raider's action warned that he was intent on making certain by filling Blake with lead before moving in to claim the horse.

No hesitation now. In one fluent motion he rolled over onto his left flank and brought the Colt sweeping up. He triggered. Above the blast of the shot he clearly heard the murderous thud of his slug slamming home. The impact hammered a Coyotero backwards over his horse's rump, his rifle pumping bullets harmlessly into the sky as he tumbled into eternity.

Lightning fast, Blake swept his weapon around to search out Taliaferro, only to find the outlaw's mount now turned broadside-on to him with the rider sliding safely out of sight down the animal's far flank. The man's foot was the only part of him visible now where it hooked up around the pommel.

Discarding the Colt, Blake snatched up the Winchester and triggered after the fast-fleeing paint. The animal stumbled and regained its balance to run on for another twenty yards before a bullet to the back of the skull brought it crashing down.

Blake sprang erect and was rushing forwards even as the swift blur that was Taliaferro was legging it away between the horse and that big blue boulder. He worked the action of his rifle to send lead whipping about the running figure. Abruptly another man, a Coyotero bobbed up close by and triggered from the hip. Blake gunned him down, then cut back to the fast-moving Taliaferro again, loosing a hail of hot lead.

The runner went charging straight past his rock, head tilted back, eyes focused on the rising sun.

The running dead man somehow continued forwards even after Blake drilled another slug into his guts. Abruptly then, he pitched headlong to tumble downslope end over end until his body was snagged by a stand of cactus, and was still.

The reverberations of the shots were still hammering in Blake's skull as he lunged back to his roan and filled leather in one bound.

Taliaferro was gone, Blake's own gun was empty. He didn't even spare a glance for the dead as he spurred away. He knew where his lead had gone. With rifle in hand, he leaned low over the roan's neck to go storming away across the flats for the ridge, riding hands and heels.

He'd covered half the distance before he spotted the thin patina of dust rising from beyond the ridge hump. His response was to whip the animal to even greater speed. He'd figured the death of two of their number might have goaded the Raider survivors to stay and fight, but that rising billow of dust told him they were crafty enough to wait it out and seek out their own time and place to fight, not play by his rules.

Hoof-lifted dust boiled around Blake's mount

minutes later as he reined to a sliding halt atop the broken-backed ridge. In the distance, the Raiders were now barely visible.

He might still have given chase had not the distant clanging of iron-rimmed wheels against stone reached his ears. Dragging his gaze away from his swiftly receding quarry, he wheeled northwards to see the wagons had turned about and were coming back.

'What the hell—?'

He'd ordered Mesquite to keep the wagons rolling westwards until he rejoined them. What the hell did he mean by ignoring orders at a critical moment by coming after him?

'It was like a mutiny, damnit!' defended the crotchety old cook when he'd caught up with them a further two hundred yards from the ambush site. 'Them damned females. . . .'

Red-faced and indignant the old-timer sucked in a huge breath as he jabbed an accusing finger at the wide-eyed girls, now staring down from their wagon.

'It was the Carmody gal what started them agitatin' first when we heard the shootin' . . . claimin' we should oughta go back to see if you was all right or not. And then the others joined in singin' that same damned song! "Save Mr Blake!" I could've—'

'And you couldn't keep a bunch of females in

line for just a few minutes?'

'I would've but for that crummy redskin.'
Mesquite glowered across at a passive Burns Red.
'He's a great help, that one. Just as soon as that
Carmody gal started in on how we should oughta go
back to rescue you, he backed 'em up. Even helped
'em swing their teams around, so he did. So there I
was. I could either come back with them or run
away on me lonesome, and I'd have looked six
kinds of a fool doin' that. Right?'

Before Blake could respond the other's indigna-
tion abruptly gave way to concern. 'You sure you're
all right though, ain't you, boss?'

Blake sucked in a breath and nodded. His grim-
ness of mere minutes earlier was fading fast by this.
He realized that but for the return of the wagons he
might well have been tempted to go on after the
Raiders, which could have proved fatal.

So it seemed they'd actually saved his life by dis-
obeying orders – though he would never concede
that point.

He knew it was high time they pushed on. But
there was one more chore to be taken care of first.

'Where is Mr Blake off to now, Mesquite?' Dixie
Todd called from the wagon seat as she watched
him whirl his prad about to go spurring back
towards the stake-out line.

'Your guess is as good as mine, miss.'

'He go to walk the Coyotero into darkness,' Burns Red stated enigmatically.

'What the hell does that redguts lingo mean?' Mesquite growled irritably.

Burns Red shrugged. 'You see.'

And see they did.

With all eyes upon him now Blake loped across to the bullet-riddled body of the Coyotero known as Chow Man. They saw the flash of sunlight on steel as Blake palmed his six-gun and angled it at the dead man's face. Two evenly spaced shots crashed out and the corpse twitched almost as though alive.

Horrified, Abigail Whitney swiftly turned her back, hand fluttering at her throat.

With smoke trickling from his Peacemaker, Blake rode across to the sprawled, dust-coated figure of the second Coyotero, and again shots sounded. Blake recognized him from long ago as Sayapati.

Silence. As every eye watched, Blake calmly reloaded. It was Dixie Todd who said unevenly, 'He hates the Raiders *that* much?'

Mesquite thrust his battered hat back with a gusty sigh. Although the old-timer had not anticipated Blake's action, he understood it only too well.

'Not hate. But Apaches believe if he loses his eyes in battle he ain't never gonna be able to find his way

to the Happy Huntin' Ground,' he explained.
'Them Coyotero Apache bucks with their eyes shot
out is gonna have to wander the dark places
between heaven and earth forever.'

'How barbaric!' an ashen-faced Abigail Whitney
whispered, as Blake started back towards them.
'Why – he is every bit as primitive as they are.'

'He never just done what he did out of cussed-
ness, Miss,' Mesquite defended. 'He's only thinkin'
of tryin' to keep us all alive.'

Abigal stared across at him. 'How could his shooting those dead men's eyes out possibly assist us?'

'He's just let the rest of that mongrel pack know
they're up against somebody who knows their ways,
is all,' supplied Mesquite. 'He hopes to scare them
off.'

'You see, Abigail,' Beth Riley said. 'I knew there
would be an explanation.'

Blake's face looked gaunt, with the skin stretched
tightly across the facial bones as he reined in
between the wagons, the women watching him with
expressions ranging from revulsion to admiration.
Yet silently each was wondering the same thing,
namely, was it possible this bloody ritual they'd just
witnessed might actually work and spell the end of
their danger, even save their lives?

That was a question not even Blake himself could

have answered with any certainty. He'd outsmarted the Coyoteros, killed two of their number then turned the weapon of their own superstitions against them in his dealing with the dead. Right now the enemy might be in full flight or they could just as easily be drawn up behind the next hillcrest preparing a bloody ambush attack.

Who could be sure? He'd done all he could.

He stretched wearily and dragged his eyes off that ridge. His gaze lingered upon Carissa Carmody for some reason before he looked away.

'All right,' he said at last, his voice strong with that familiar authority. 'We've got miles to go before night. Head them around and let's get rolling.'

CHAPTER 7

WAGONS WEST

It was a little after noon and brutally hot when the sudden appearance of the riders sent the feeding buzzards flapping and cawing into the sky.

The Coyotero Raiders ignored the scavengers as they reined in to sit their saddles in silence, staring down upon the claw-and-beak-mutilated dead.

The faces of the trio were clouded with superstitious dread as they saw what the white-eyes had done to Crow Man and Savapati. But the face of Coyotero Mad Wolf showed only seething rage and it was a long moment before Big Body found the nerve to address him.

'Thinking of what befell Crow Man and Sayapati,'

he enunciated carefully, 'might it not be well to forget the white women now and ride in search of easier prey?'

Mad Wolf spat in the dust. That was Big Body's answer. All understood it. Mad Wolf would not quit now, which meant nobody would, or could.

As soon as he digested this, Big Body, the loyal lieutenant, reluctantly accepted that they should continue in pursuit of the wagons. There would be no further talk of quitting, for Mad Wolf never backed off once a decision was made. They would hunt the white eyes and drink his blood . . . just as soon as this burial chore was attended to.

There were many prayers. For the white-eyes had blinded the slain braves' bodies and the only hope of the living for the dead men's salvation now lay in their ability to invoke the spiritual aid of the Great Coyote in their name. Should Great Coyote hear and heed their call he would emerge from his lair in the Mist Mountains, seek out the wandering blind spirits of Sayapati and Crow Man, then gently guide them to the Gates of God and thus save them from the dread fate of wandering the Dark Places through all eternity. . . .

Standing on the western side of the biers with arms lifted to the sky, his deep voice droning on through the seemingly endless litanies and incantations, Mad Wolf made an imposing figure.

The mourners paid no heed either to the squawking buzzards or punishing sun.

Their concentration was absolute – until Mad Wolf himself was suddenly distracted by something in the sky. All turned their heads in the direction he was facing to glimpse the faint wraith of dust rising upwards.

To the Indians the desert was a book they read every day of their lives, and what they saw in that dust was all too clear. It was not a dust devil, nor something kicked up by a desert antelope, but plainly a cloud raised by the hoofs of horses. And after a long moment's study, hawk-eyed Spotted Eagle was able to improve even upon that considerable feat of identification.

'The horse hoofs wear steel,' he grunted to Mad Wolf. 'They are the horses of white-eyes!'

'Now you take that Carmody gal,' Mesquite Mick invited as he guided his wagon across yet another seemingly endless stretch of salt pan. 'That is the only one I can't really figure in that bunch. There is somethin' about that handsome filly that jest don't set square with me, Mr Blake, no sir, don't set square at all.'

The oldster turned towards the tent flap. 'You listenin' inside there, Mr Blake?'

Blake was trying his best not to. Sprawled out upon one of the mattresses that were wedged in amongst the sundry bags and boxes of supplies crowding the wagon, he'd barely managed to grab a couple of hours rest during that long hot afternoon.

Yet judging by the feel of gritty eyes and heavy limbs, he still needed more of the same before he would feel recovered from the past forty-eight hours which had seen him barely close his eyes. He might have had a chance of achieving that if a gabby Mesquite wasn't making rest impossible.

He faked a snore but the cook recognized it for what it was and went right on talking.

'Yessir, perplexin' little piece that there Carmody gal, Mr Blake. Pretty as four aces but seems to me she's got a whole mess more on her mind than jest romance and orange blossom, yessir. Now, you take the way she was talkin' when they was all gettin' confidential back at Dragoon Springs couple of days back. . . .'

The voice droned on. Blake groaned inwardly. He'd already heard every detail about the girls and their prospective husbands, even if he didn't give a damn if they married miners, dudes – or short-order Mexican hash-house cooks. Mesquite had already covered these unlikely possibilities himself, but seemed intent now on widening the infinite world of speculation.

Blake could have ordered him to be quiet as he gabbled away up there upon the high seat were it not for the fact that he suspected Mesquite feared he could be lying down there worrying about Raiders or Injuns, should he reveal he was still awake.

But eventually he was forced to sit up to knuckle at his eyes and run fingers through his hair. He hipped around to squint irritably through the rear flap. The late afternoon glare struck sharply at sore eyes as he sighted all four girls clearly visible upon the high seat of the wagon following behind.

This meant that the canvas-covered section of their wagon was empty. . . .

'. . . Not that it's none of my business, I know,' Mesquite was prattling on several minutes later, 'but I got me a powerful hunch that this Carmody gal did recognize the name of Beth Riley's feller back at Dragoon Springs, Mr Blake, even though she claimed she never did. Now that struck me as mighty curious on account. . . .'

The man broke off to turn his head in order to see if his audience was paying attention. The wagon was now empty! Mesquite cursed and sawed on the reins and was starting to holler when Dixie Todd called from the canvas shade in the wagon behind. 'It's all right, Mesquite. Mr Blake has decided to keep us ladies company a little way.'

'Now what the tarnal would a man want to go and do a thing like that for?' Mesquite complained, gigging the mules on again. 'If he was tired of talkin' to me he only had to say so.'

The wagons rolled on towards twilight like big-hipped, happy girls. Burns Red was still breaking trail, while in cool canvas shade Blake continued to sprawl luxuriously alone upon Dixie Todd's mattress. The girls' chatter didn't disturb him any here, yet sleep continued to elude him, and he knew why.

Raiders.

He reassured himself that even if those scum were tailing them they wouldn't dare launch an open attack by daylight. In addition, this wide-open stretch of semi-desert was hardly suitable for ambush. Therefore this had to be the right time for him to to spell up some in preparation for whatever they might have to deal with before they put the last of the desert behind themselves and reached the safe and plush green oasis of Dragoon Spring.

Although mostly able to doze off any time he chose, Blake soon found that self-discipline wasn't functioning properly today. So he killed time thinking about the girls, pondering on how far they'd travelled already and how much farther they had yet to go.

They were damn good travellers, he would concede now, even if he would not deny that upon meeting up with them in Archangel his first impression had been of four rather foolish, flighty and impetuous females united by chance in a common cause. But in the intervening time they had shown a strength and toughness not expected. Until occasionally now, Blake the bitter loner, actually found himself wishing only the best for them upon reaching Tincup.

Especially Carissa Carmody, he thought, for some reason he didn't understand . . . yet. . . .

At least he was certain that those hardy miners and sundry hardcases who peopled the lush and well-protected gold-mining camp out there would ensure the party would be as safe from harm in Tincup itself as if they were back in the city, once they arrived.

But they still had long miles to put behind them before that part of their dream became reality.

A sneer touched the edges of his mind at that thought. Dreams! He used to dream once . . . never did so now. . . . Or maybe he'd dreamed that one day . . . but surely that was impossible.

He exhaled, slung one arm across his eyes against

the light probing through the canvas and shrugged. He wanted the lurching of the wagon to rock him to sleep yet was still wide awake when one of the girls came through from the front.

His irritation showed as he propped up on one elbow, but he quickly relaxed. For it was Carissa Carmody. The girl appeared dusty and wan-looking towards the end of the long day, with soft auburn hair clinging to her cheeks and neck with perspiration, yet she still managed to look a million bucks to his weary eye.

Wondering what she wanted, Blake continued to stare up at her in silence for almost a minute. Then to his astonishment the girl knelt at his side and touched his face with a cool hand.

'You need sleep, Mr Blake,' she said quietly. 'Let me help you doze off. . . .'

His powerful hand closed over her wrist. The grip hurt, but the girl made no sound. The testy side of Blake wanted to order her to get the hell away from him. He wanted to show he was a man who'd been reached by a woman's tenderness once, but never could be again.

Instead he said nothing until at last his fingers unlocked, leaving their impression in her soft skin. His eyes suddenly feeling strangely heavy-lidded, he allowed them to close over and was aware of a sense of great calm stealing over him almost immediately. It was with a keen sense of pleasure that he felt her fingers trace lightly and soothingly across his forehead until all his tensions began to ease. His last conscious thought was of his dead wife before he drifted off into a deep and healing sleep.

It was the first time he'd ever been able to think of her without pain. And somewhere, mysteriously, he experienced something like a return of his old gentleness, a sense of hope. . . .

The girl remained by the sleeper's side as the miles rolled slowly by, humming snatches of tunes while brushing away the occasional intruding insect that wanted to disturb his rest.

The terrain was rapidly altering as sundown approached. Throughout the punishing afternoon the caravan had worked and lurched its way stolidly across the vast white saltpan known as Jackson Flats. Yet now the entire landscape was slowly turning red as they entered yet another sweep of torn and broken country. Reddened and scaly earth replaced the saltpans and once again there was cactus, tall and aloof.

Burns Red had not been given specific instructions by Blake before he had taken up occupancy of the other wagon, but the young Indian knew he would be expected to awake him by sundown at the latest. But when he came searching through the second wagon he encountered unexpected opposition. Carissa informed him that Mr Blake was resting and nobody was permitted to awaken him – then bossily shooshed him out and on his way.

It was a full hour later before Burns Red and Mesquite agreed it was time to halt and make camp. They figured the wide-open saltpan country they'd been crossing ever since daylight to be safe enough here against the possibility of attack. To have attempted to press on through such remote country at night, with Blake still asleep, seemed simply too risky.

The girls readily accepted the decision to camp and almost tumbled down from the wagon's high seat, showing marked signs of exhaustion.

Mechanically, they set about the by-now familiar procedures of setting up camp, and so weary were they that it was some time before they grew aware of the dark and uneven shapes of the mountains looming against the sky ahead. Puzzled, they drew the rugged hills to Mesquite's attention, giving the oldster an excuse to pause in his chores and air his knowledge of the outdoors.

'No mystery,' he grunted. 'They've been there all day only we couldn't see 'em for the haze until night turned it dark.'

He spat a stream of tobacco juice and added casually, 'Them's the Cochise Mountains.'

Suddenly, the girls weren't weary any longer. Their destination, Tincup, as they had learned, lay at the foot of the Cochise Mountains. During the day they had drawn within actual sight of their landmark without realizing it.

'Now, simmer down, girlies,' the old-timer felt obliged to warn. 'Them there moutains what look so cool and welcomin' are a hell of a lot further off than they look right now. We ain't gonna get there until—'

He broke off as the flaps of the women's Conestoga parted and Blake emerged. He squinted up at the moon uncomprehendingly for a moment and everybody got ready for an explosion as he scowled darkly then jumped to ground.

Why in hell had they let him sleep so long? Didn't they understand the dangers of travelling this country without a proper lookout, namely himself? he demanded. And so on.

He didn't spare anyone, not even Carissa Carmody whom he seemed to hold responsible for coaxing him off to sleep in the first place. And once he'd got all this off his chest and went striding off to climb a lookout rock – 'To make sure we're not surrounded by Injuns or Raiders or whatever the hell else' – as he put it, they realized the testy Mr Blake was just being himself again.

But in reality a change had taken place in this once sombre man of the wilds. A greater change than he could ever have expected.

CHAPTER 8

DEVIL'S OVEN MOOD

The pale light in the east expanded slowly into an ever-strengthening glow which eventually ushered in the great golden disc of the Devil's Oven moon as it swung free of the earth.

The first full flood of light bathed the four figures grouped around the bodies of the dead Coyoteros lying on their backs with their faces to the moon.

The headstrong Orford and Simeon had wanted to ride down and investigate the bodies when they were first sighted, just after high noon. But Chan

Nero had urged caution and was supported in this
by black-bearded Maitland Gwyn.

By the time they'd sighted the dead, these hellers
who had been trailing the wagons every burning
mile from Archangel, were in sore need of rest.

Chan Nero elected to make camp then and
there, and so the bunch had spent the entire afternoon spelling in the shadow of a draw before
making ready to ride down to inspect the dead
upon dusk.

Nero stood now with his long snout crinkling at
the stink of death and rancid fat while his companions warily inspected the bodies. Earlier, the
hardcase leader had been tempted to pass by this
grisly scene here to the south of the big canyon, and
push on after the train.

But the wary habits learned from life on the
owlhoot prevailed, and had seen him hold to his
original plan. If there were two dead men out here
on this desolate strip of Devil's Oven dirt, he wanted
to find out how they'd died and why, if possible.
And certainly and most important, did they have
friends who might still be alive? Dangerous friends,
would likely prove a sound guess.

The desert-wise Nero was well aware that Raider
packs had roamed the Devil's Oven for several
years. He wasn't about to risk blundering into that

kind of danger without conducting a reconnoitre first.

Having determined the Coyotero Apaches had been slain with six-gun and rifle then had their eyes blown out, Gwyn, Simeon and Orford began hunting for clues. Nero, meantime stood smoking a black cigar and gazing across the landscape.

The killer found the chill night wind invigorating and the tobacco tasted fine. It was now beginning to seem to him as if they might not have to worry over much so far as Apaches were concerned.

According to Lang Simeon, who had conducted a close inspection of all sign, the bucks killed by Blake had been survived by two henchmen who'd taken on the responsibility of erecting their death biers before heading off west.

If the boys found nothing more now, the outlaws figured to push on west after the train, free of the fear of a bunch of howling Coyoteros bobbing up from behind every cactus bush along the way.

Feeling better by the minute, the killer flicked his cigar butt away. It landed just a few feet distant and, as it bounced briefly before finally coming to rest in the dust, Chan Nero saw the earth move before his startled gaze.

The section which had plainly now raised an inch, was roughly four feet square. Nero blinked groggily and pinched his eyes with thumb and fore-finger. What the hell was wrong with him? Too much sun – or not enough booze? It must be the heat, he decided finally, and when he opened his eyes again he saw the section of earth that had attracted his attention now appeared as featureless and normal as its surrounds.

He massaged his brow. Surely, only a touch of the sun could cause a man like him to start seeing things that weren't there?

But there was nothing wrong with Chan Nero's eyesight, nor had the brutal desert heat scrambled his brains. For that little square section of earth had indeed moved, just as two other similar sec-tions immediately in back of him were lifting right now.

Nero finally saw these ominous slits appear beneath the slow-raising platforms, yet could not make out the hostile eyes staring out at him from the dark recesses of the covered ambush pits which the Raiders had dug for concealment hours earlier.

Only the tigers of the desert possessed the guile and skill to set up such an ambush in featureless terrain like this. Only such as they would have the inhuman patience required to remain crouched and unmoving for so long in a hot, airless hole in the earth beneath a pitiless Devil's Oven sun. Waiting. . . .

And likely only the feared nomadic Apache band with the Raiders could kill with such murderous swiftness.

Orford and Simeon died within a heartbeat of one another as the rifles suddenly roared from the ambush pits with the thunder of the shots so shatteringly loud and close that Maitland Gwynn and Chad Nero were for the moment deafened.

That brief moment was all the time it took for Red Paint and Spotted Eagle to explode from their holes, screaming like madmen and swinging their rifles like clubs.

Chan Nero managed to get his six-gun clear of leather before Spotted Eagle's sweeping rifle butt crashed against his shoulder with brutal force. Nero reeled backwards and grabbed for the Bowie in his belt at the back. He saw Gwyn go down under the overhanded thump of an Apache rifle butt, and next moment the lean, corded arms of Mad Wolf had snapped around him, imprisoning his arms against his chest.

Nero was a powerful man and in that heart-stopping moment a desperate one as well. With the adrenalin pumping blood and urgency through every artery in his body he ducked his head, flexed his legs, then attempted to burst his way free with sheer strength.

Mad Wolf's locked hands showed no sign of breaking their grip.

The Apache waited until Nero's first explosion of energy was expended then fiercely increased the pressure of his bear hug.

Nero instantly felt his senses begin to reel as he struggled for air. He glimpsed the lean red shapes of the other Apaches now seeming to dance in his vision and a terrible curse erupted from his lips.

To no avail. His big head was snapped backwards suddenly and Mad Wolf's contorted features seemed to dance in his vision.

The stink of a long-unwashed body clogged Nero's senses and the instinctive tenor that every westerner harbours for the Apache seemed to drain him of his last dregs of strength.

He felt his knees buckle and the world was turning dark. So this was dying! Strange ... but he'd always imagined he might quit the world with honour and all flags flying, with brave companions urging him on.

Instead he was being crushed by a stinking Apache in the middle of a hostile desert and didn't even understand the reason why.

In those last moments before losing consciousness, Chan Nero, the killer who had sent so many men into eternity with his roaring guns, knew proudly he was not afraid.

It seemed a long time after that before he opened his eyes to find himself staring at the moccasined feet directly before him, and realized they hadn't killed him after all. He'd been spared, but the knowledge that he was still in the hands of the murderous Raiders of the desert filled his veins with ice and a greater terror than he'd ever known.

It was almost dawn and the night creatures of the Devil's Oven were surrendering their nocturnal kingdom to the coming day as Jackson Blake rode towards the campsite.

The roan blew softly through its nostrils and jingled its bridle chains as a light pressure on the reins brought it to a halt.

Building the cigarette he'd denied himself over the past hours spent scouting their backtrail, the rider forced himself to relax in the saddle, man and horse forming an integral part of the awakening landscape surrounding them.

With the light of the sunrise directly in back of him Blake pushed on down the gradual slope to be greeted by a predictably splenetic challenge from

Mesquite, who stood by his wagon struggling to drag suspenders over his shoulders.

'You wouldn't think of stoppin' a moment to inform a body you might be gone half the dad-blasted night, would you, Mr Blake? You wouldn't give a second thought about how much frettin' and worryin' folks might be goin' through, would you?'

Blake calmly halted his mount and surveyed the campsite located at the base of a giant red butte. Burns Red was coming down from the high hump where he'd been standing watch. The only girl visible thus far was Carissa Carmody who stood brushing her hair at the tailgate of their wagon as she watched the sun rise.

He headed for the remuda with a few short words: 'You can light the fire while I roust everyone out – and make sure my coffee's hot!'

Mesquite Mick McGuire blinked. 'Did you say light a fire?'

'Right. We need grub and hot coffee before starting off today.'

The transformation in crotchety Mesquite Mick Maguire was astonishing as he went hustling off to find something to burn. There hadn't been a single fire lit in three whole days. Not only did Blake's order now mean they could have their first decent hot meal in too long, it also told Mesquite something he really wanted to know. Namely, that for the present at least the boss man reckoned they were safe from danger.

Over coffee, after the Indian had come over to assist with unsaddling the roan, Blake furnished Burns Red with a brief summary of his night's scout.

He told how he'd covered a broad area of their backtrail several miles wide and deep without sighting sign of Apache or any other danger.

He didn't bother informing Pima about that distant cloud of dust he'd glimpsed moving from east to west two hours earlier. He reckoned that whoever it might have been it had almost surely not been Indians. For if the Apache was still interested in them, he would make certain-sure you wouldn't know about it.

Or Raiders, maybe. Who could tell?

The women questioned him closely over breakfast a half-hour later. Were the Coyotero Apache still following them or had they quit after that shooting yesterday? His replies were terse. He continued munching tasty flapjacks with four pairs of eyes fixed on him, nodding reassuringly in response to further queries while in reality he was far less sure. This was mainly due to memories of past experiences with the Coyoteros, which no man could ever forget.

Yet despite some uncertainty Blake felt well pleased with his early-morning scout by the time he'd crossed to the fire to get a second mug of coffee. He mentally dismissed the Indians for the time being to concentrate on the day ahead.

They'd made good time and had luckily remained remarkably free of setbacks . . . so far. Earlier travellers had nicknamed this waterhole Old Reliable, with more than a suggestion of irony. Its banks were littered with the skeletons of birds and beasts, testimony to the fact that Old Reliable could turn just as unreliable as any desert water source in the dry season.

Fortunately, there was water that day and soon they were underway again, toting enough water to get them to Salvation Creek, providing they used it sparingly.

But Carissa Carmody made no secret of her suspicion that Blake's only motive in announcing the stringent cuts was because he drew some perverse pleasure out of making their journey as uncomfortable as possible.

'You know that is ridiculous, Carissa,' Abigail disagreed mildly.

'Of couse it is,' supported Dixie Todd, tilting her hatbrim low over her eyes against the strengthening glare. 'That's just the man-hater coming out in you, honey.'

132

'They're all the same!' came the terse response.

'I surely just can't understand how anybody as young and lovely as you could ever get to be so bitter, Carissa,' Beth remarked, holding a kerchief against her nose to ward off the dust rising from the teamers' hoofs.

'I don't believe we're meant to understand, Beth.' Dixie glanced at Carissa. 'You are determined to keep your secret to yourself, aren't you, honey?'

'Well, perhaps I was . . . but if you're all so determined to throw yourselves away on whatever breed of nobody with enough gold dust to pay for us – and call it love – then count me out.'

'So, you're prepared to go through with what all of us are, honey,' Abigail smiled, 'only it's the words that bother you, like love and eternal devotion. . . .'

They wrangled for a time – that was easy enough to do during the boredom of the seemingly endless journey. But soon they were on their way. Blake had no intention of travelling too far in such heat and his objective that day was to attempt to reach Salvation Creek by midday, where he intended waiting out the worst of the afternoon glare.

He felt that a combination of luck, good leadership and the whole-hearted co-operation of the women had managed to get them this far. He was confident that if they could reach Salvation Creek without mishap, and find the water flowing, they would make it all the way.

Blake was checking out the trail immediately ahead on foot, when he glimpsed the faintest stir of movement a long way off across the salt. Frowning, he climbed a low mound for a better view. He was able to determine some stir of life out there but there was no telling what it might be without binoculars.

Rejoining the wagons, he borrowed Mesquite's battered old army issue field glasses, then clambered atop the cook's wagon to study that far-off smudge of colour and movement.

Burns Red came across to join him curiously while the women watched from the shade alongside their wagon.

Blake's features were grim when he finally lowered his instruments. He flipped them down to Mesquite, then jumped down, knees bending to cushion the impact.

'Everybody stay put here,' he ordered, heading for his mount. 'Don't move until you get my signal.'

'What was all that about?' Dixie Todd called across to Mesquite as Blake forked his cayuse and rode off.

'Seen somethin' out there, so he has,' Mesquite

muttered, fiddling with the adjustments on his glasses. He put the instrument to his eyes, worked the screws some more as he squinted west, swore feelingly. 'Goddamn, what'd he do to these fool gadgets? I still can't see what in hell is goin' on.'

'My eyes are a little younger, Mesquite,' Dixie said, joining him. She held out her hand. 'Let me take a look-see.'

The old cook fiddled with the glasses some more, swore a little, then passed them to the girl as she climbed up beside him.

Dixie set the instruments to her eyes, then worked the adjustment screws.

Blake's figure immediately jumped large in her vision and she swung the glasses to scan the wastes ahead of him. Suddenly her hands froze and the others heared her sharp intake of breath.

'Well, don't keep us in suspense, dang-bust it all!' Mesquite complained irritably. 'Can you see what that is out there, or cain't you?'

There was no colour in Dixie Todd's face as she lowered herself to the high seat. She nodded and licked her lips. 'Yes . . . yes, I saw it,' she whispered. 'It's . . . it's a man's head!'

CHAPTER 9

MERCY IS A BULLET

The man had been buried up to his neck in a deep salt drift. His eyes were empty sockets crawling with ants, the skin of his face burnt raw by a murderous sun. Blake could tell by the formless babble coming from his mouth as he attempted to speak that he had also lost his tongue. He was a breathing dead man.

It was an hour since Blake had ridden on ahead of the wagons. It had taken time to draw within gunshot distance of that slowly twisting head after it first caught his attention. He'd first spent some time circling the area in case of a trap before closing in on the grisly remains of what had once been a powerful man.

The Coyotero Raiders had left little sign behind yet to his expert eye it was more than enough. He'd guessed Raiders upon first sighting the victim through his field glasses, and his subsequent sign-reading had merely affirmed that fact. There had been four in the party and the prints told him some were identifiable as members of the bunch he'd tangled with way back at Murphy's Canyon.

He dismounted and approached the victim, the big Peacemaker still angling from his fist. He wasn't concerned with the why or what he was confronting, only the how.

It was plain that the Raiders had overtaken his party then forged on ahead. That would have been simple enough to do, he reckoned, due to the fact the scum were travelling lightly laden astride fleet-footed and desert-bred mustangs as opposed to the plodding progress of the wagons.

The thought struck that the enemy might have bypassed him yesterday afternoon while he'd dozed in the rear of the girls' wagon. . . .

Then he remembered.

That puzzling, far-off cloud of dust he'd glimpsed on the horizon last night! It hadn't been deer or antelope, but rather the desert scum passing and leaving them in their dust!

Scum – plus one – he corrected himself, as he stood wide-legged staring down at the mutilated creature before him.

Revulsion stirred, yet he forced himself to look at what had once been a man. He had always reckoned the desert Apache the most cruel and murderous an enemy a man might encounter. But these Coyoteros with the Raiders left simple and savage Indians in their dust.

And knowing the killers wouldn't have been content with simply taking tongue and eyes here, he knew that were he to begin digging and scraping he would find the victim's private parts gone, his belly slit open – not severely enough to kill him quickly – but only to make the death longer and more agonizing.

Coyoteros? Surely, they rated a far uglier name than that.

It was physically painful to lick his lips and draw his six-shooter. He realized the mutilated man could still hear when he plainly twitched at the soft metallic click of Blake's piece being cocked. The ruined head turned slowly in Blake's direction and the moaning ceased to give way to an expectant silence.

The man could not speak and his eyes were gone. Yet he managed to convey a terrible pleading that could not be mistaken.

'Kill me!' those sightless sockets begged. 'Mercy!' screamed the soundless tongue.

The Colt came up slowly to reach firing level and it was only when he was taking careful aim to make certain the first bullet did its deadly work, that Blake realized the man's mutilated features were familiar. This was Chan Nero's henchman, Maitland Gwyn. The last time he'd seen him had been from his lookout position that night at Buzzard Gulch.

'Take it easy, friend,' Blake murmured. 'And *adios.*'

The shattering blast of the Colt .45 was the last thing tough Maitland Gwyn heard in life.

'It jist don't make no kind of hoss sense no matter which way a man looks at it,' Mesquite Mick complained around a bulging jawful of chaw tobacco. 'They bust their insides gittin' ahead of us across this damned desert, they musta had at least a dozen good chances to try and jump us – but what do they do? They carve some poor varmint up, stick him in the dirt where we can't help but sight him, and then skedaddle. Now don't try and tell me that makes any kind of sense.'

'Is always reason,' grunted Burns Red from astride his pony plodding along at the Conestoga's rear wheel.

Back in the white man's world the simple young Pima was at a disadvantage, yet out here in the dust and heat and the smell of death, there was a sureness and confidence about everything he did.

He glanced across at Blake riding a horse-length forward of the off-wheel. 'Always reason when Coyotero Raiders do something. Is this not so, Blake?'

'Right,' came the grunted response as cigarette smoke drifted over Blake's shoulder.

'Then what *is* the jumped-up Judas reason why they done it then?' the grizzled cook demanded in exasperation.

Blake and Burns Red traded looks across sweating mule rumps. Old Mesquite had them there, for though they'd had ample time to do so by this, neither had yet figured how Maitland Gwyn had come to end up buried to his neck in a saltpan drift with his life's blood slowly leaking away in the savage heart of the desert.

But who ever *really* understood what could and did happen in the desert?

They weren't destined to gain any further insight into Raider hearts and minds until after they

140

reached the lava ridge.

Several miles in length, this massive wall of ancient lava reached far out across Fortitude Valley from the Boiling Fork Hills, now lying beyond the horizon's rim to the north.

In some sections the lava had been entirely swallowed up and obliterated by the endless winds, the salt and the sand. Yet directly dead ahead of the wagon train now the geological phenomenon loomed in some places an intimidating fifty feet high, the tortuous twists and coils of its massive bulk appearing to the eye to have cooled but yesterday and not a thousand years earlier as was the reality.

The ridge was one of the wonders of the desert country yet the party offered it no more than a cursory glance before moving on to top out a rise in the trail which revealed something else of interest standing in clear sight before the ridge a quarter-mile distant.

Something chilling.

White Raiders and Coyoteros stood by their sleek mounts in clear sight a hundred yards distant, seven chillingly impressive men and all seemingly between twenty and thirty years old by the looks, Blake had heard the wasteland killers were white men and red men together, as this pack plainly was. At first glance the only hint of threat about them

141

were their weapons. Each man had two or three Colts hanging off his belt; each held his mount's lines in one hand while the other rested on a gunbutt.

As taut moments ticked by the ranks of the gunmen suddenly parted and Jackson Blake saw what the Raiders had been concealing.

It was a white man immediately identifiable as Chan Nero.

The hardcase had been stripped to the waist and lashed to a man-sized cactus. They couldn't see the jagged spines that pierced his back but knew they were there. Nero's big head snapped up sharply when the man who appeared to be the leader suddenly slammed him in the belly with his rifle butt. He howled in pure agony, the sound seeming to hang in the hot air a long time before fading to a whimper.

Blake's expression didn't alter but he was raging inside. The Raiders' appearance en masse was a jolt and he could feel the danger in them like heat coming off a hot iron. Everything about that pack held menace – their impressive appearance no longer meant a damn thing. These well-mounted desert riders were the real butchering kings of the badlands. A man had only to look at their prisoner to know that.

142

But what in Hades did they want?

Abruptly two of the party – the taller one plainly the leader – gigged their mounts forward some distance before halting by a broken blue boulder. The leader raised his right-hand palm forward, then formed a fist and struck his chest.

He wanted to parley.

The watching women showed alarm when they saw Blake knee his mount forward, amazed by the way he appeared so calm and in control in the face of such obvious danger.

But Blake was neither of these things. Yet nobody would ever guess at his tension as with Burns Red at his side he continued on to rein in before the Raider.

He'd already made his appraisal of the leader yet the closer he got the more menacing the man appeared. His face was young but the pale blue eyes were very old and cold. His partner was an ugly Coyotero, liberally marked by countless vicious knife scars. Blake assessed them as young-old men who'd likely seen too much death not to be both unchangeably scarred and visibly aged by it.

'I'm Farley and this is Mad Wolf, but I'm doing the talkin',' the man with the dangerous eyes announced, and proceeded to do just that.

He first emphasized the obvious, namely that the

Raiders had already demonstrated they had the numbers and strength to wipe out the wagon train by force if they wished. He went on to insist there was no need for their situation to be resolved that way, however, particularly when a bloodless solution offered itself.

Farley the Raider was ready to trade.

He would turn Nero over to Blake and in return Blake would simply deliver two of the women. The redhead and the blonde were Farley's choice. He presented his proposal with some confidence due to the fact that he'd originally planned to take all the females, but had moderated his claim in the hope of making a deal without bloodshed.

Blake nodded slowly to himself when Farley fell silent with arms folded across his barrel chest to await his response.

Less than an hour earlier Mesquite had been insisting there seemed no motive behind the Raider attacks. Yet Blake understood those reasons only too well now. There was no doubt in his mind what would befall Nero if he refused to trade. He was offering the life of a white man for two white women while adding the inducement that the girls would not be harmed in any way.

But the strongest shot the Raider had in his locker was as yet unnanounced. That was the obvious threat that should Blake fail to do a deal, everybody could well wind up exactly as had Maitland Gwyn. Even the women!

The choice was Blake's; the life of Nero in exchange for Carissa and Dixie. Failure to do the deal would result in Nero's death and likely his own.

Deliberately Blake rolled a quid of saliva around his mouth then spat it squarely between the forelegs of Mad Wolf's mount in a manner that couldn't be misinterpreted.

Mad Wolf's features darkened ferociously. His right hand snaked towards gunbutt but froze when Blake slapped hand to his Colt. The Raider's chin came up and his black eyes glittered.

'So be it!' he hissed. 'Next time we speak it will be in words of blood!'

This was no idle boast and Blake knew it when Chan Nero had begun to howl again before they got back to the wagons. He was still screaming at sundown three hours later.

Noting the effect these cries were having on the women, Blake reached a decision. As soon as darkness fell he snaked away from the camp alone with his rifle. His intention now was to get within rifle range of that giant barrel cactus and finish Nero off. But as he glided through the eerie desert gloom there came a sudden change in the torture victim's cries. The prolonged howls rose higher and higher and seemed to last an impossible time until cut off as abruptly as though someone had thrown a switch.

Silence.

Blake waited long minutes before rising and slowly returning to the wagons. . . .

Sometime later when the desert moon peered over the rim and its cold metallic light flooded a hostile world, all got to see why Chan Nero had quit screaming.

They'd split the man from neck to crotch with their knives, leaving the carcass impaled grotesquely upon a giant cactus. Of the enemy now there was no sign. It was as if the night had opened up and engulfed them whole.

Blake couldn't ignore the chill in his veins as he slowly turned his back upon the grisly scene, yet this began to ease when the faces of his companions emerged from the shadows. The girls appeared shocked and jaded, with even the resilient Dixie Todd appearing close to tears. Burns Red and old Mesquite were putting on brave faces but with only partial success.

But what he had seen had its effect, and Blake was soon changing his own plans. He knew his people could no longer be left alone. He would have to take them along with him, which meant they should all best get moving. Like, right now.

There were tears and protests when he gave the orders to move on. But this was a Blake in fighting mode whom they didn't really know, stern and uncompromising. The party was shortly under way, some weeping, others cursing, yet each subconsciously aware that but for Blake's harsh authority, each or maybe all of them might have fallen apart like something fashioned from wet straw.

While hidden eyes watched and cruel minds made plans. . . .

The journey seemed to grow worse as night wore on. Already the mules were starting to labour when Blake ordered a brief rest. With no intention of pushing too deeply into this valley by day, his objective now was the sanctuary of White Bird Canyon where he planned to wait out the coming day's worst heat.

He planned on continuing on at mid-afternoon, travelling right through the night and he hoped to reach their destination of Salvation Creek by the middle of the day.

CHAPTER 10

DESTINY

'Mr Blake!'

'What?'

'I'm gettin' cramp.'

'Then stretch and hush!'

He listened until all grew quiet again in White Bird Canyon. But not for long. For rugged Mesquite Mick was genuinely scared for one of the few times in his life, and it showed.

'Mr Blake!'

'What now, damnit?'

'You really reckon them Raiders will come after us?'

'If I didn't believe it do you reckon I'd have

waited here listening to your bellyaching for three hours? Sure, I do. Now hush up!'

Blake sounded his usual gruff self, yet underneath the tough exterior the first twinges of doubt were starting to nag.

It was almost midnight the following night and they'd reached White Bird Canyon several miles south of Salvation Creek at around nine. Close to their ultimate destination – and yet so far.

As usual Blake had done his figuring while they travelled, calculating just how long Farley and Mad Wolf might wait at the water before realizing they had passed Salvation Creek by. And then, figuring forwards, he estimated how much time it would take the enemy to reach White Bird Canyon should they give chase, which they surely would.

He'd laid his plans carefully when concealing both Conestogas in a deep box canyon branching off from White Bird. He'd then returned afoot to the narrow canyon entrance with Mesquite and Burns Red to set up their ambush, if needed.

The rocky south entrance to White Bird provided a perfect natural ambush site and Blake had confidence in it. When and if the enemy showed, they were sure to be more focused on simply hunting down their quarry than the possibility of ambush.

It was only with the chill midnight wind blowing

149

down the canyon and the cramp of inactivity creeping into his bones that he began to wonder if he'd underestimated the enemy. If that was the case then the Raiders could be making their way around the canyon that very moment – and ready to attack.

Tension gripped at him but he fought it off by blanking his mind and permitting instinct to take over.

And instinct assured him he'd guessed right in figuring out how things might unfold.

A cold, tense slab of time dragged by. And then he heard it. Somewhere in the night, unshod pony hoofs were drumming in the direction of White Bird Canyon.

'Burns Red!' he called softly to the dim shape above and off to his right.

'I am ready, Blake!'

'Mesquite!'

'Ready, by God! Goldurn it, but it must be a real pain to be right *all* the time like you—'

Blake ignored the sarcasm and thumbed back the knurled hammers of his big twin Colts and focused upon the narrow band of moonlight higher upslope where the horsemen would first appear.

He was a man who'd made almost a religion of his isolation and independence, yet had a feeling now that all manner of people seemed to have penetrated his armour since he'd ridden from Archangel, seemingly an eternity ago.

Could this mean he was softening up? Or maybe even growing vulnerable? And should this be the case, might it not in turn indicate he could at long last be recovering from the loss of his wife?

This thought came as a jolt. And yet when he concentrated, it was with a sense of wonder and immense relief to acknowledge that somewhere along this trail he had at long last come to terms with reality, had finally farewelled the woman he'd loved and lost and had felt filled with a great sense of peace ever since as a result.

It was as if this Devil's Oven crossing had proven exactly the cure required to relieve him of that three-year burden of regret and get on with his life.

Strange that his thoughts should be taking that track right now, he mused. But maybe this was simply because he knew the moments ahead could prove to be the most uncertain and unpredictable of his life. And in a sudden flash of comprehension he saw just how many assorted people he had unawares allowed to draw much closer to him than he'd realized on this journey. Mesquite, Burns Red, Dixie Todd . . . Carissa Carmody. . . .

Carissa Carmody?

He found himself picturing Carmody's face and

the way she had looked at him before he'd quit the wagons just now. It was almost as if she cared genuinely for him and his safety.

The girl's image held vividly until dark riders loomed abruptly into sight against the skyline a hundred yards to the east. . . .

Mad Wolf and his Raider masters made no concession to caution as they swept down the long, boulder-scattered gradient giving into White Bird Canyon.

The Indians with their leader at their head had set a relentless pace ever since discovering the wagon train had bypassed Salvation Creek.

Blake knew the redskins were still after him and the white women, but they now also had a blood score to settle. For he had bested Mad Wolf at every turn and had even made him appear a fool in the eyes of his own band at Salvation Creek.

The Coyotero was now hungry for blood and spurred on by lust. Even so, he still rode clever and was watchful every inch as the hoofbeats of their unshod ponies rose to echo against the shadowed walls of White Bird Canyon.

Yet not even the hawk eyes of a Mad Wolf could pick out the motionless figures spread belly-flat amongst shadowed boulders, where Blake's party

had found time to find positions of good camouflage. Gun barrels had been dusted to ensure
against giveaway glitter, every precaution taken. To
Mad Wolf and the dog pack trailing him there was
not a single indication that this rough stretch of
trail might be different from any other they'd
already crossed since quitting Salvation Creek.

Their first hint of danger was when a lance of
rifle fire erupted from shadowed boulders and tall
Red Paint threw up both arms, screaming just the
once as he crashed lifeless to the trail.

Mad Wolf was staring ahead with wolfish intensity
when that single shot snarled. Reacting instinctively,
the Coyotero killer hurled himself headlong down
the off-side of his mount to cling on by one hand
and foot, briefly working his rifle and shooting back
before he tumbled to earth – while a thunderous
volley erupted from above.

Yet lightning fast as Mad Wolf's response had
been, Blake's was even quicker. His twin Colts
churned like the drums of doom as the killer Indian
squirmed his way frantically behind cover where he
tucked his ugly head in tighter than a sleeping sage
hen as the rider hurtled by.

Blake was hunting for another target when a
bullet from Big Body screamed off rock mere inches
from his face to pepper his cheek with rock slivers.

Instantly he dropped and swung guns towards the looming figures of horse and rider. Mesquite's weapon chimed in and Big Body was slammed from his saddle, triggering aimlessly as he fell.

Blake heard the moan from Burns Red's position but dared not risk a glance. The whole scene was chaotic now with Mad Wolf's dead mount blocking off the trail and Big Body wounded but still shooting. Red Paint lay sprawled in death while Spotted Eagle worked the action of his flame-belching Winchester repeater from the back of his rearing horse.

And Mad Wolf's rifle beat heavy thunder from the gloom.

Blake concentrated his fire upon Mad Wolf and moments later from the corner of his eye saw his man crash down, spewing crimson. Mesquite howled triumphantly from his left, then swung his smoking rifle upon Spotted Eagle. A split-second later, Blake felt lead bite his thigh like a white-hot iron. He flinched, staggered, gritted his teeth then sent a volley of shots back at the Indian until his hammers clicked upon empties.

He was hurling the empty Colts aside and reaching for his rifle when Mad Wolf charged headlong. The Apache came over his dead mount and hurtled towards Blake's position with the swiftness of a

154

hunting puma. Blake's hands closed over his rifle but as it came sweeping up the Coyotero leader launched himself in a prodigious dive that carried him over a huge grey boulder to crash into him with stunning impact before he could start in firing.

The two men rolled in a mad whirl of dust that carried them downslope headlong into the canyon wall with stunning impact.

Blake was hurting but that didn't slow him any. Three brutal blows hammered into Mad Wolf's contorted face before the Indian hooked a muscular leg up beneath Blake and tripped him backwards. Fast as death, the Apache brought his swinging knee into the side of Blake's skull, sending him spinning onto his back.

Through a dizzying haze Blake saw his adversary snatch up a gun. Too fast, Blake dived under the shot, rolled, knew he could not double back in time to take an advantage – then sighted the revolver lying at his feet.

He snatched it up and triggered. His first shot was wild but Mad Wolf was thrown off-balance by the thunderous report. Then the Indian was lurching at him, but not fast enough as Blake made his inexorable way forwards through roiling smoke and dust – deliberate as destiny.

He triggered at point-blank range and the dusty,

lurching shape that was Mad Wolf went down with a soft rustling sound against the earth.

Blake staggered erect to stand there swaying for a long minute unmoving and with dust coiling about his tall figure before a bewhiskered head raised slowly from behind rocks close by. 'Judas, Mr Blake, it looks like we done it. You all right?'

Still unable to speak, Blake nodded and gazed about him. The air was thick with the smell of blood and lifeless figures littered this place of mortal combat. Yet he felt no pleasure or triumph, indeed seemed to feel nothing at all until he heard the voice.

'Mr Blake!'

He swung at the cry and the dim figure appeared through the haze. Next moment Carissa Carmody was in his arms and it seemed the only safe and comforting place to be in all this violent land – and was.

They had all reached Tincup feeling more dead than alive. But such was feminine vanity that the first thing they wanted to do when they learned their suitors were waiting for them across at the rickety hotel was to find some place where they might prepare themselves before their all-important first meetings.

Carissa was first to be ready after sprucing up at the Widow Brown's, but the others weren't to be left behind, and soon all were streaming across one of the roughest streets in the West for the hotel where big bronzed men were eagerly waiting, while an almost-smiling Jackson Blake puffed on a stogie and watched from the sidelines.

'Sure do look happy, eh, boy?' Mesquite asked.

'Sure enough . . . or at least all but that one yonder.'

'Huh? Which one?'

Blake indicated the slender, handsome figure of the girl all reckoned as the prettiest and likely even the smartest of the whole group. 'The good-lookin' one there, Carissa Carmody. Dangest thing. The beauty of the bunch, and would you believe her pen pal got cold feet when he knew we was comin' in, and took a runner.'

'The hell you say! Y'know, she looks pretty perky, don't you reckon? For a lady what's just been stood up, I mean,' commented Mesquite.

'Guess she does . . . matter of fact she looks real cheerful – even if she is stranded to hell and gone out here now.'

The tall figure of the man who'd brought them safely across the desert was today looking very different. Blake was smoothly shaven, freshly bathed and appeared remarkably smooth and relaxed for a man with weeks on the trail behind him. He strolled casually across to Carissa Carmody who, seated now in a rocker, glanced up and smiled at his approach.

'Miss Carissa.' He tipped his hat. 'I, ah . . . heard what happ—'

'It's perfectly all right, Jackson. Actually, I feel freer than I've done ever since I was talked into this foolishness by the girls.' She gestured. 'They're all making wedding plans already. I know I'd have died if my man had been here and felt he had to propose.'

Blake almost moved on. It was in him to do so. But something stronger caused him to pause to study her with his level gaze. He felt great that morning. The escort had been a strain, but he was proud it had come through safely. And it was a journey and an experience he knew he would never forget, for somehow just over the past twenty-four hours, with the success of the escort guaranteed, he'd realized so much had changed. It was as if the ghosts had finally left him, that his lost love was no longer a burden but a gentle friend who was releasing him to live his life as he knew he should, not in the past, but now.

And suddenly, studying Carissa, he remembered an invitation he'd received to visit the local spread of a friend, which he'd intended to ignore . . . until now.

The journey was over, he felt better maybe than he'd done in years . . . she was smiling in the sunlight.

He tested her with a serious, 'Well, goodbye, Miss Carmody.'

'Go with God, Mr Blake,' she responded, and he caught the glimmer of a tear.

That was enough. Sober-faced – for this was still his way even when he was feeling fine, as right now, he removed his left foot from stirrup and extended a hand.

'I'm visiting friends,' he said. 'They've invited me to stay over on their spread for as long as I've a mind? Would you. . . ?' He paused to clear his throat. He was rusty. 'Would you care to join me?'

He patted the horse's silken neck and managed another grin – surely a record for him. She stared up at him, poignantly uncertain . . . until he reached out and took her hand. She swung up behind smoothly and gracefully as if she'd been doing it all her life, and it was something he would never forget when she wrapped her arms about his waist and pressed her cheek against his back.

Together they rode from the town and headed for the cool high country.